FOR LOVE AND ITALIAN

LIZA MALLOY

Dear Aunt Ann —
This book doesn't exactly
match my college experience
(in any way) but I did love
my foreign language classes.
Happy reading! ♡ Liza Malloy

This book is dedicated to all who study and teach foreign languages.

"The limits of my language are the limits of my world."
  Ludwig Wittgenstein

* * *

"A different language is a different vision of life."
  Federico Fellini

CHAPTER 1

BRIDGET

I was fully immersed into the best dream I'd had in ages when a soft whisper fluttered in my ear. I was strapped to the back of a super hot Navy Seal, about to jump from an airplane when the murmur grew louder. I swatted in the direction of the voice, determined to return to my hunky rescuer, but a sharp clicking sound pierced into my subconscious.

I pried my eyes open one at a time to see my best friend Stella.

"I'm not going to wake you anymore if you try to hit me," she snapped.

I groaned and smashed the pillow against my face. "I was just in the middle of a dream."

"Let me guess—you were kissing Valentino?"

I giggled, despite the fact that the hit song would now be stuck in my head for the rest of my crazy Monday. "No, but there was a hot guy involved."

I shoved back the covers and hopped off the bunk. My bed was in the far corner of the cold dorm in our sorority. Because roughly twenty of us shared the same room on any given night, alarms were strictly prohibited and the house's newest residents were tasked with waking us upperclassmen. Normally the system worked, but on important days, I needed someone I could trust. Stella fit the bill perfectly, and it wasn't a burden to her since she woke early almost every morning so that she could do yoga. I'll never know how I became so close with a morning person, but that was really her only flaw, so it was tolerable.

We trekked upstairs to the small living space we shared with two other Juniors, grabbing our shower caddies before heading to the bathroom. I fit all of the sexist girly stereotypes when it came to my morning routine—super long shower, slow and meticulous process of drying, straightening and styling my long hair, followed by equally tedious makeup application. It literally took me so long to get ready some mornings that I downed multiple cups of coffee before reaching the final step—accessorizing.

I lived in awe of the girls who could roll out of bed, brush teeth and hair, throw on clothes that they hadn't even set out the night before, and head out the door in under fifteen minutes. These were probably the same girls who looked cute after a soccer match or enjoyed trendy hobbies like camping or rock climbing.

Stella was ready before me, so I tossed her a small wrapped package.

"You got me a present?"

"It's the first day of classes and I wanted you to feel loved," I said.

Stella plopped onto the papasan chair and ripped open the paper. I watched in the mirror as her excitement morphed into confusion. "You wrapped up my day planner?"

I giggled. "Yes, but flip through it." It had taken me nearly two hours the previous day, but I'd written in the birthday of every major celebrity Stella stalked on social media. I'd also penciled in a few spa days for the two of us, which was the real present since we'd use my credit card. Well, my dad's credit card, actually, but whatever.

Stella's grin widened with each page until finally she popped out of her seat. "You are the bestest bestie ever, you know?"

I shrugged. "You're pretty sweet yourself. Okay, which necklace?" I held the two options up in front of my top.

Stella rolled her eyes and swiped the shorter one out of my hand. "We already decided last night you would wear the longer one. No day-of changes." She set it on my desk. "Besides what's the big deal? It's the first day but it's not like we're new to the school. Everyone already knows you."

"Not necessarily, and it's never a bad idea to make a good first impression." I grabbed my sunglasses and purse and started to the door. "For all you know, I might meet my soul mate today."

"Pretty sure if he's really your soul mate, he won't write you off based on a bad necklace choice."

I paused, aware that Stella was staring pointedly. "What?"

"Your backpack. Think maybe you'll need that?"

I snatched it off the floor and we walked to campus together.

I was pretty excited about my schedule this semester. I still had one Friday class, which was a total drag, but it couldn't be avoided. It was a French conversation class that met five days a week and was required for my major. Plus, I'd finished all of my general education requirements, which meant all the remaining classes I'd be taking throughout my college career were subjects that actually interested me. Today, and every Monday and Wednesday, I had French conversation, Italian, and a French literature class. On Tuesdays and Thursdays, I had French conversation, French grammar, and a Shakespeare class. Given the lack of math, science, or other lame subjects in my schedule, it was sure to be a great semester, regardless of my Friday schedule.

OWEN

My nerves caught me off guard that morning. Now that I was in my sixth year of teaching, it should've all been routine. As a full time PhD candidate, teaching was a critical component of my life. The teaching credits were a requirement for everyone seeking a doctorate in Italian, but we were paid for the work, which offset the tuition. This semester I was teaching three classes, a 100 level course and 2 courses at the 200 level.

These early courses were a mixed bag. On the one hand, lots of the students at that level lacked any real desire to learn Italian and were simply trying to cross off a general education requirement needed for their degree. In each class though, there were some students with a genuine interest in the language, and watching their passion grow was the most rewarding part of teaching. Another perk of teaching at this level was that the students were unlikely to notice if I made a slip in my pronunciation or grammar.

I'd finished all of my own coursework in Italian needed for my diploma, but was still finalizing my dissertation. I was scheduled to present my thesis in early November. My focus was on the benefits of using technology to simulate immersion in a country and provide virtual tours to enhance fluency in students. I felt like a sham whenever I sat down to write, since I really believe that students should actually live amongst the people in order to truly learn the language and culture. But, there was a sizable chunk of research supporting my thesis, so I wrote what I needed to say to increase my chances of earning one of the few, coveted professorships in the Italian department of some university.

Each semester as a graduate student I'd audit one course in a different subject, and, having minored in French, I was taking a graduate level French course this year. It was a literature course based on Creole novels, which received rave reviews. I was excited about it, if only because it was the last time I'd ever fill the role of a student at a university.

My phone buzzed as I headed into the eight-story limestone building. I glanced at the text, sent from my twin sister Olivia.

She wrote, "good luck today. But even if you're nervous, don't picture the students in their underpants. I hear that's frowned upon."

Laughing, I wedged my phone into my pocket. Olivia was my only sibling, and as twins, we'd always been close. Nowadays, she was a speech therapist in the suburbs about three hours away. Olivia spent most of her days teaching toddlers better enunciation, while I was surrounded by college students with alarmingly similar behavior to toddlers. We often commiserated about the tension between the desire for full independence and the absence of maturity necessary to truly act independently, an affliction which struck both of our sets of pupils.

One of the tricks I'd learned for staying on track with class was to wait until right when class was scheduled to begin before entering the classroom. This avoided tempting the students with an opportunity to discuss their work outside of office hours which inevitably resulted in a delayed start to class. But on the first day of class, I always made an exception to my self-imposed practice. On the first day, the minutes before class offered an invaluable predictor of what my students would be like.

I knew that old saying about not judging a book by its cover, but I still felt my first impressions of students had proven pretty accurate in the past. I foresaw that the ones who arrived early and began looking at their textbook would be decent students. The ones who arrived early and began flipping through the textbook for another class would be even better students. And the slackers who rolled in right as I was ready to start, looking like they'd slept in their clothes, well, they rarely surprised me either.

As I watched my second year Italian class stroll in on that crisp September morning, I filed away my snap judgments, having observed a couple students who fell into each of the usual categories. Less than five minutes before class began, though, a student caught my eye. She was gorgeous, with long dirty blonde hair and a body like a centerfold, but it was her shoes that actually attracted my attention initially. Despite being on a college campus with old, cracked sidewalks, where nearly everyone walked everywhere, this girl wore strappy metallic colored high-heeled shoes that likely cost more than my monthly teaching stipend. The rest of her outfit looked similarly pricey, from the fake diamonds decorating the side of her jeans and the long sparkly necklace on top of her navy blue tank top. Although we were indoors, she wore oversized black sunglasses.

I glanced at my roster, briefly wondering if she was an actress or some other pseudo-celebrity. None of the names rang a bell with me, so I watched the rest of the students, gauging their expressions. Every male in the class was watching this same girl, practically drooling, and the girls all seemed a tad annoyed by her. The girl paused, taking in her options for seats, veering towards the section where the well dressed, jock-type guys sat. I mentally pegged her as the popular high school cheerleader type, probably a decent student but too shallow and too entrenched in the mean girl tactics to ever reach her true potential.

But then she turned, choosing a seat off to the side of the classroom next to a shy-looking guy who had quite possibly never spoken to a girl in his life, let alone a hot girl. I braced myself for something appalling to come out of her mouth, but instead she smiled and turned to him.

"Did you see that hit last night at the top of the seventh inning?"

The guy gazed up at her, his expression so comically confused that I nearly laughed out loud.

She gestured to his royal blue Cubs shirt.

"Oh," he said. "Yeah. It was awesome."

She sunk into the seat beside him. "I know, right?" She wiggled her fingers in front of him, and I realized they were painted blue with what appeared to be tiny Cubs logos on each one. "It was so perfect that I had to go get my nails done last night to show my support. Even though it took so long that I didn't get to bed until an ungodly hour."

The guy still looked petrified but had started to relax.

I, for one, was thrown. From my comfy seat at the front of the room, it actually looked like this girl had intentionally sought out the lonely guy. Had I seriously been that wrong in my judgment?

The two jocks I had thought she'd sit by quickly moved over by them.

"Is that why you're wearing the shades? Thought maybe you were just hungover."

She lifted her sunglasses, revealing striking green eyes. "It's possible there was some celebrating last night. You can't not celebrate a win like that, right….." she paused, turning to the quiet guy beside her.

"Mark?" he said uncertainly.

"Good to meet you Mark. I'm Bridget. Us Cubs fans need to stick together."

"I can cheer for whatever team you want, girl," the taller guy said, slinking into the seat beside her.

She shook her head. "That's not how team loyalty works. Jerrod, Dan, meet Mark. Mark, that's Jerrod and Dan. They liked the White Sox until the Cubs won the World Series. Again."

Jerrod and Dan smiled and shook hands with Mark. Somehow, this gorgeous girl had not only befriended Mark but had seemingly caused his perceived worth to skyrocket in the eyes of the other guys, too.

As fascinated as I was by this entire conversation, it was time to start class.

I stood and cleared my throat before introducing myself in Italian. I turned to write my name on the dry erase board, and as I swiveled back to the class, Bridget caught my eye and smiled widely, batting her thick, dark eyelashes. Maybe I hadn't been wrong about her after all. She had *trouble* written all over her.

The class was uneventful, and I left confident that they would be a decent batch of students. I trekked upstairs to my office for my proscribed office hours, though having just distributed the syllabus listing those hours, I suspected no students would drop by. I downed my sack lunch at my desk, finalized and printed the syllabi for my other courses, then made my way back downstairs for my one student class.

The French literature course was a graduate level course, so the small group of students were primarily graduate students. There were only fifteen of us total, and I recognized ten others. Italian and French were under the same general department at the university, so I wasn't surprised that most of my classmates were familiar. The remaining three must be undergraduates majoring in French and the last student hadn't yet arrived.

The Professor, Madame Chabaud, entered, and right behind her was the girl from my morning class. Bridget. She looked flustered, but quickly slid into a desk and pulled her books and a notepad from her backpack. I glanced over, but she didn't seem to notice me.

I enjoyed the class, Madame Chabaud having launched right into her discussion of the first book. The topic fascinated me, as I'd always enjoyed learning about the interplay between history and literature. But from a skill level, I was lagging behind the others. I was nearly fluent in French, but the Creole dialect was just varied enough to completely throw off my translations, and Madame Chabaud's Haitian accent was a stark contrast to the traditional voices of the professors hailing from France itself.

I glanced over at Bridget once more during class, curious if she recognized me from Italian class, but she quickly turned away, her expression unreadable. Apparently I wasn't as memorable as she was.

CHAPTER 2

BRIDGET

Stella and I met for sushi that evening to rehash the day. Stella went first, having endured much more drama in her day thanks to not one but two ex-boyfriends in a single class. By the time she finally turned to me, we were almost done with three of the four rolls we'd ordered to split.

"So, did you actually meet your soul mate today?" she asked.

I sighed wistfully. "Decidedly no. There weren't even any hot guys in my classes. Well, except..."

"I thought you said Jerrod and Dan are both in your Italian class," Stella interrupted pointedly. "They're both hot."

I shrugged. "They are. And I agree they're both cute enough, but definitely not soul mate material."

"Why not?"

"They're kind of jerks."

Stella pierced a sliver of ginger with her chopstick. "So they're exactly your type."

10

She had a point. Historically, every guy I was attracted to ended up being a complete asshole. But still, best friend code dictated she not remind me of that. I returned to my earlier thought.

"You never let me finish what I started to say. There was actually one hot guy today, and he was in two of my classes. Well, sort of."

"How is someone 'sort of' in a class?"

I leaned forward, signaling that what I was about to say was risqué. "He was a student in one of my classes, and he was teaching another."

Her eyes widened. "Oh do tell more."

"My Italian professor. I guess he must be a grad student or something. He looks older but not that old. And totally hot. So then when I went to my French lit class, the creole one, he was in the class."

"You're sure it was the same guy?"

"Oh yeah. I wouldn't forget that face. Or that butt."

She giggled conspiratorially as I maneuvered the last bite into my chopsticks.

* * *

TUESDAY'S CLASSES were similarly uneventful, and by Wednesday, my mind shifted to the weekend. There was a football game Saturday afternoon, which meant Stella and I would be tailgating all morning. Saturday night was a back to school bash that our sorority co-hosted with the same fraternity every year. The party was guaranteed to be a blast, but I hadn't actually decided on a date yet. Normally, I wouldn't hesitate to go stag, but my ex, Patrick, would be there. I was not about to show up dateless when he'd surely be all over some bimbo the whole night.

After Italian class, I walked to the student union building.

I plowed through some little homework before focusing on the important task at hand— finding a date for Saturday. I made a list of possibilities, highlighting the pros and cons of each. When it was time to head over to my French class, I snapped a picture of the list and texted it to Stella so I could get her input.

I made sure to arrive early to my next class, since I'd actually walked in after Professor Chabaud on the first day. The reading had taken me forever the previous night, but I enjoyed the book so far. The Professor talked to the class for a few minutes and then divided us into groups of three to discuss a series of questions about the first half of the book.

I turned towards the students she'd grouped me with, then blushed. Apparently, I was going to spend the next half hour speaking French with my Italian professor. I smiled lamely and glanced down at my notepad, unaccustomed to the sudden shyness overcoming me.

"Bridget, right?" he said suddenly.

I nodded.

"I'm Owen and this is Kristin."

Kristin launched into the first topic while I was still deciphering Professor Chambers' words. He acted like he didn't recognize me from class, but he knew my name. What could that mean?

Fortunately, I didn't have long to dwell on it. Kristin was clearly a graduate student of French, so her spiel took infinitesimally less time than it would've taken me to formulate even a single coherent thought on the text. Luckily, Professor Chambers chimed in next, and I made a brief comment third.

Madame Chabaud began speaking again with about ten minutes left to class, but we'd left our desks pushed together in our small groups. When class ended, I tried to think of something witty to say, hoping to show my Italian professor that I wasn't a total slacker. But when I stood, my notepad slipped to the ground, and the paper I'd torn out to text to Stella slid several feet away, right under Professor Chambers' desk.

He bent and picked up the paper, glancing at it casually. He opened his mouth to say something, then simply laughed.

I could not even envision a more mortifying scenario than my professor seeing my list of potential dates. I snatched the paper, wadding it into my backpack while feeling my face burning with humiliation.

"Not Jerrod," Professor Chambers finally said, clearly still struggling to stifle his laughter.

Apparently, I had been wrong. My professor weighing in on my list of potential dates was significantly more embarrassing. I considered the strong possibility that I'd now need to drop both classes simply to avoid the continued mortification.

"It's for a friend," I mumbled, hightailing it out of the room before I could further humiliate myself.

OWEN

The next two weeks of classes went smoothly. This wasn't surprising, since my students generally didn't start to panic until midterms, when they realized how little they'd actually worked up to that point. My predictions about which students in my 100 level course were most promising had panned out so far, and my gut feelings about the slackers proved true as well. Bridget, however, continued to stump me. Her work—both in my class and in French—was impeccable, as far as I could tell. She was a natural with the languages, but it was clear that she studied hard regardless.

In my Italian class, she continued to politely engage with

the kids I generally wouldn't consider very popular, but she also had no problem flirting shamelessly with the jocks in the bunch. By this point in the year, most students stopped putting so much effort into their appearance, but Bridget still arrived at each class in pristine clothes, with perfectly coiffed hair and accessories that matched her outfit. Even her nails were flawlessly maintained, with the color or pattern changing weekly.

It looked like a lot of work. I wondered why someone who was clearly smart and nice felt so compelled to spend so much time on her appearance, especially since every male for miles was already fawning over her.

Kristin, the third person in our French lit group, dropped the class the second week. She was due to present her dissertation the same month as me, and I guess she was just too busy for one more class. Even though she was by far the strongest member of our group, I wasn't terribly sad to see her go since this would offer me more time to figure out the enigma known as Bridget. I didn't imagine it would be awkward, but then Madame Chabaud assigned us a group project that would require us to meet with our partners outside of class.

I considered inviting Bridget to my office, but decided that might make her uncomfortable, so we agreed to meet at the library instead.

BRIDGET

After the mortifying incident involving my potential boy-toy chart, I was hopeful that Professor Chabaud would mix up the study groups in our lit class. Instead, she forced us to do a project out of class. Further complicating matters was the fact that thanks to the fluent girl dropping the class,

Professor Chambers and I were now the only members of our group.

We met at the library to work on our project, and rather than continuing to stress over the awkwardness of the situation, I opted to address it head on.

"This is a little weird," I said.

His dark blond eyebrows narrowed. "How so?"

I blushed, wishing he'd understood without explanation. "You're my Italian professor, but you're my classmate in French."

He shrugged and flashed a half smile. "I can't be a prodigy in every language."

I chewed the inside of my lip.

He finally glanced down. "I'm not a full professor yet. This is my last year as a graduate student and assistant professor. I present my thesis in a few weeks and keep my fingers crossed someone hires me as an associate professor."

"So why are you taking Creole?"

"As an undergrad, I minored in French and Spanish. I can take classes outside my focus area as a graduate student, and it sounded fascinating." He paused. "Even though I'm not exactly soaring through it, I have no regrets about taking this class."

I smiled, starting to relax.

"Besides, I should be asking you that question. I'm a PhD candidate taking a post-graduate course. Why is an undergraduate like you taking a graduate level course?"

"It sounded interesting."

"Are you struggling as much as I am?"

I hesitated. "It's the hardest class I've taken so far, but French is my major."

"You're only a Junior."

I frowned, wondering how he knew that.

"Class roster for Italian," he explained, reading my mind.

"It's really not awkward for you, studying with one of your students?"

He shook his head slowly. "It might be different if you weren't such a mature student. I don't think I could study with…" he paused, clearly tempted to list names, then stopped.

"Nevermind," he said. "Let's get this finished."

CHAPTER 3

OWEN

First semester was flying by, and I dedicated every free moment to my thesis. It was fully written and formatted for publication, but I still had the oral presentation. As if that weren't enough to stress about, the department head was observing my teaching in each of my classes.

Bridget was friendly with me now, both in my class and in our shared French class. She'd initially seemed so timid when we were first placed together as study partners that I wasn't sure it would work, but we actually made a surprisingly effective team on the assignment. She was quieter in French, presumably because she was one of the only undergraduate students, but when she did speak up, she always contributed something meaningful to the discussion.

In Italian class, I continued to be fascinated by her charisma. Bridget was a true leader among her classmates, though possibly not for all the right reasons. Her chipper attitude helped halt some whining from the class, and one day she actually convinced more than half the class to dress in Cubs colors for good luck on a game day.

I recognized that it wasn't normal for me to think about an undergrad as much as I was, but I chalked my preoccupation with her up to the fact that I was in the midst of a serious dating dry spell. Having spent my summer teaching in Italy, then being too busy with my thesis to date since returning to the Midwest, it had been too long since I'd had any romantic involvement.

The dating drought was new for me. Since seventh grade when Katie Hullman agreed to go with me to our town carnival, I'd never had a shortage of women in my life. I wasn't a total player, but there'd really only been one serious girlfriend ever. Even though our breakup six months ago had been my idea, I hadn't really jumped back into the serial dating game I played before I'd met her.

Once my dissertation was over, I'd prioritize my personal life. But in the meantime, I was running late to meet Bridget to finish our project.

BRIDGET

Owen and I met one more time to finalize our project. Normally he was enthusiastic and focused, which made it easy to fly through the project, but tonight it was obvious his heart wasn't in it.

"You seem distracted," I blurted out. "Is everything okay?"

Owen glanced up slowly, his gorgeous eyes like wide pools just asking me to dive in. "Uh, yeah. I, well, I present my graduate thesis tomorrow. So I guess my mind is sort of focused on that."

"Tomorrow? Seriously? Why are we speaking French then? Do you even need a good grade on this?"

He scrunched his eyebrows. "Well, no, but you do, and I'm your partner, so…"

"I can finish the rest of this on my own tomorrow. No worries," I said.

Owen looked skeptical, so I added, "Really. You're just slowing me down."

That earned me a chuckle.

"Can I hear it?" I asked.

"Hear what?"

"Your thesis or whatever. Don't you need to practice?"

"Umm…yes, but it's in Italian."

I shut my notebook. "Okay, so I'll follow along as best I can. Just pretend I'm the department head or whoever you have to talk to tomorrow."

"It's the entire department," he said.

Yikes. That seemed intimidating. But I shrugged casually, playing it off like I already knew that and it wasn't a big deal.

"You sure you want to hear this? It's long."

I nodded. He pulled some notes from his messenger bag, gazed up again, then began. I hadn't actually heard him speak Italian like this before. In class, he never said more than a sentence or two, and then he always spoke very slowly and used basic words. Now he was speaking quickly, at a cadence that sounded natural and authentic. I had no clue what he was saying, but the accent was pretty hot. Over the next fifteen minutes, I picked out a few dozen words I recognized and from that, concluded his thesis was somehow related to teaching.

When he finally stopped talking, he confirmed my suspicion, giving me a summary of his thesis in English.

"Well, I'd give you an A plus," I said.

"You understood all that?"

"Not even a little, but it sounded very doctoral."

He laughed. "I wasn't too nervous about it all until I heard there's a tenure track teaching position opening at the university for next semester."

"Here? In the Italian department?"

Owen nodded. "It's a long shot. Most likely they'll hire a native speaker, possibly with more teaching experience, but I'm hoping the fact that they already know me might work in my favor."

"Wow. Good luck," I said.

"Grazie," he replied, winking.

Just then a woman appeared outside his office. Owen jumped to his feet, smiling as he went to her. They hugged with a familiarity that made me oddly jealous. It didn't help that she was beautiful, with dark brown hair and eyes nearly as bright blue as Owen's.

"I thought you'd be back at your apartment by now," the woman said.

Owen gazed over at the clock. "Sorry. I should've texted you." He turned awkwardly back to me. "Bridget, this is Olivia, Olivia, Bridget."

Olivia smiled warmly and shook my hand, but I noticed the suspicious glance she gave him as she turned.

"Bridget was kind enough to listen to my presentation," he said. "She's in that French lit class I told you about."

Olivia turned to me again. "Do you speak Italian also?"

"Solo un po'," I said.

"Good pronunciation though," she said, only somewhat patronizingly.

"I have a good professor," I said, suddenly feeling a tad nauseous. "Well, I better go. Good luck tomorrow."

OWEN

Olivia stayed and listened to me practice for hours. Having spent some time during childhood with our Italian grandma,

Olivia had a decent grasp of the language. She couldn't speak it fluently, but she understood what I was saying and was prepared with a series of questions to challenge me like the other professors would in the morning. When I finally reached the point where any additional practice would just stress me out, we took a break to change into pajamas and grab some snacks.

Olivia's presence truly helped with my stress level, so I appreciated her making the trip, especially since I wasn't exactly the best host. She could only stay two nights, but I figured tomorrow we'd go out to celebrate the presentation being over, whether it went well or not.

Olivia and I had both attended the same university for undergrad, and she'd met Dave, her husband, there. They married two years after graduation and had moved a short distance from our hometown. Her husband wasn't the type of man I'd imagined her ending up with, but as long as he kept making her happy, I had no complaints.

"So, Bridget, huh?" Olivia said suddenly, jolting me out of my thoughts.

"What about her?"

"Seems weird that you were studying for a class you don't even need when you could've been focusing on your dissertation."

"I needed a distraction and she's a French major, so the grade does matter for her."

Olivia's eyes narrowed and in that instant, I hated that I knew exactly what she was thinking. "She's in one of your Italian classes, isn't she?"

I nodded.

"She's quite pretty," she said, goading me.

"Is she?"

Olivia chucked a kernel of popcorn at me. "You know she is. She's gorgeous."

I shrugged. "I think she's dating half my students."

My sister clearly didn't believe me but she chewed another handful of popcorn before replying. "Just be careful," she finally said.

I frowned.

"I know, I know. You would never do that," she said.

"Then why caution me?"

"Because I can read your mind and you needed to hear it out loud. Besides, I saw the way you looked at her."

"I didn't look at her any particular way. You're the one who's enamored with her beauty."

Olivia smiled at this. "True." She sipped her tea. "She's not your type anyway."

"Oh?" I said, unaware that I had a clear cut type.

She shook her head. "She's too perfect."

I considered that statement, but before I decided whether or not I agreed, Olivia stood.

"It's late and you have a big day tomorrow. Go to bed. I set a billion alarms on my phone so no worries about oversleeping."

I smiled, nodded, and watched her retreat to the extra room before switching off my light and heading back to my own room.

* * *

I SLEPT TERRIBLY THAT NIGHT, and my presentation was even more grueling than I'd imagined. All of my colleagues and professors sat in a half circle in front of me, along with a couple dozen other graduate students and faculty, and stared at me, expressionless, while I spoke. Their faces were so blank that at one point, I even questioned whether I was speaking the right language.

When I finished my prepared lecture, they pounded me

with question after question. By some miracle, the more inquiries I fielded, the more at home I felt with the material. After a while, it seemed to just naturally come together and flow.

When it was done, the department head smiled widely and nodded, a sign that I interpreted favorably. Olivia attended the entire thing and agreed that my presentation was unanimously well received, but I discounted her opinion for the clear bias. Despite that, we went out for a fancy dinner, paid for by her husband, then celebrated with drinks.

I wouldn't fully relax until after I received the official feedback, but in the meantime, it felt good to be carefree and gossip with my sister.

BRIDGET

After class on Monday, I stayed late to talk to Owen.

"How did it go?" I asked.

"I think well, but I haven't yet received any formal feedback." He paused, stacking up his papers.

I followed him as he started towards his office. "I feel bad about keeping you so long working on the dumb French project."

"No, don't. I needed a distraction. Did it, um, get done?"

He unlocked his office and motioned for me to head in.

"Yeah. I have it with me if you want to proofread."

"I trust you," he said.

"So, I'm curious about this whole thesis thing. I'm considering grad school in French eventually, so how does it all work?"

Owen gave me a brief run-through of his experience since graduation. I didn't want to appear naïve, but I really hadn't realized it took that long to finish grad school. It seemed like a lot of work. It was interesting hearing about his classes though, and how he felt about teaching the first time he tried it. He told me generally about his experiences teaching in Italy too, which was cool. That, of course led me to ask him about the study abroad options at the school.

Owen seemed more than happy to chat longer, but then he glanced at his watch.

"Sorry. Am I keeping you from some work?"

He shook his head. "No, but my office hours are over now and I was going to pick up a sandwich before heading to French class. Care to join me?"

"Sure."

We walked over to the closest campus deli while still chatting. I ordered a salad and he chose a sandwich, and then we sat in the corner and kept talking. When the conversation lulled, I brought it back to his thesis again. I couldn't imagine putting years of work into a single presentation. Stress was not good for my complexion, and I already needed a spa day to recover after every midterm or final exam I took. For a thesis, it would probably take a full spa vacation to calm me down again.

By the time we'd finished eating and started walking towards our French class, I was already dreading my own thesis, assuming I eventually got to that point in grad school.

"So did your, um, girlfriend sit in on your presentation? What did she think?"

Owen tilted his head, a thoroughly perplexed expression on his face.

I immediately regretted bringing up the girlfriend. I didn't even know what I was thinking. It was none of my business what my professor did with his girlfriend.

"I'm sorry," he finally said, shaking his head, "My…"

"No, I'm sorry. I just assumed. I meant, um, that woman that came by after we were studying. Olivia, I think?"

Owen laughed out loud. "Oh geez. Yeah, she did sit in on the presentation and she thought it went great."

That stupid pang of jealousy returned.

"But Olivia is my sister. Twin, actually. I am in between girlfriends."

He said the last part with an odd twitch of his lips. I turned down to my feet, feeling the heat return to my cheeks.

Thankfully, we were nearing the building so neither of us felt compelled to say anything else. I waved awkwardly to a few sorority sisters, former classmates, and other acquaintances and then we reached the classroom. I sat, and Owen stuck his bag on the desk beside me. I turned and realized he was laughing.

"What?"

He shrugged. "Nothing. You just seem to know a lot of people."

I wasn't sure if that was a compliment, tease, or simple observation so it took me a moment to reply. "I try to be a friendly person," I finally said.

He nodded, then focused his attention on his phone until Professor Chabaud arrived.

CHAPTER 4

OWEN

Fall semester was flying by. Midterms came and went, and I survived the dreaded meetings with students protesting their grades.

Determined to follow through with my pledge to get back into the dating scene, I asked a woman out on a date. She was a local, not a student or teacher, and she worked in an art shop, so I thought it was a fair bet to take her to a poetry reading followed by dinner. Apparently, this was a colossal misjudgment of character, as she yawned audibly multiple times during the poetry reading, then grimaced at the food at dinner, claiming the Korean dishes looked "too ethnic."

As I retold the evening with all the full gory details to Olivia over the phone the next morning, she laughed hysterically at my expense.

"Thanks for the unwavering support, sis," I replied.

"Oh, come on, you know I'm teasing. But really, I think your efforts are misguided."

"How so?"

"Well, when have you ever sought out a woman to date?"

I considered her question. Really, I guess the answer was never. Historically, whenever I'd hooked up with a woman, it was because of mutual attraction and flirting that just led to something else.

"So you're saying I should just back off and just wait for the perfect woman to fall into my lap?"

"Yes," she said, laughing again so I couldn't be sure she wasn't still mocking me.

Until this mystical perfect woman materialized in my life, there was plenty for me to do on campus. I read some books on teaching, applied for a summer teaching position abroad, and amped up my workout regime. I even set aside time to socialize with other graduate students and teachers within the French and Italian department. Now that I was on the job hunt, I needed to focus on networking more.

I also still spent a fair amount of time with Bridget. Though we no longer needed to study together for French, now that the group project had concluded, she hung around during my office hours and we chatted casually about the class. On Monday before Thanksgiving, we somehow stumbled into a debate about two of the books we'd read as part of the proscribed curriculum. She loved the novel I hated and found the one I'd preferred dull and unoriginal, but the discussion itself was precisely what made me love academia so much. Nowhere else would I hear a passionate defense of what I still say was a pretentious story.

When we weren't disagreeing about the caliber of the assigned reading, Bridget and I chatted about other random things. In an environment where most people were burned out and disgruntled, her positivity was invigorating. I started to think of her as a friend as well as a student. I was ashamed at how harshly I'd judged her at the start of the year, so much so that I pledged not to stereotype my students next semester until at least the second or third week of class.

BRIDGET

"Okay, spill!" Stella said, leaning forward conspiratorially in anticipation of the juicy gossip that I simply didn't have.

I shrugged and cautiously sipped my coffee through the hole in the plastic lid. Stella and I hadn't returned to campus early enough the previous night to catch up, so we were taking advantage of the break between our late morning Monday classes to debrief each other.

Stella had already regaled me with tales from her adventurous Thanksgiving break. Compared to Stella, I was downright tame. Still, I knew she wouldn't give up until I described my weekend in great detail.

"Start at the beginning," she said.

"Well, I had dinner with my family after I unpacked Wednesday and then I went to the local bars with old high school friends," I replied.

"And?" she asked.

"It was nice to catch up with people. Also, it was vindicating to see which of the mean girls succumbed to the freshman fifteen."

Now Stella smiled, seemingly entertained with my catty gossip about girls she didn't even know. But her expression quickly changed.

"That sounds fun. So why do you look bummed?"

I gnawed a bite off my bagel, buying myself time to consider the question. I usually felt pretty good about myself at these informal reunions, not having gained any weight since graduation and actually having even better hair and skin at present than in high school, now that my hormones had stabilized. This time, though, I'd been a little self-conscious about the lack of boyfriend.

Well, not even so much the lack of boyfriend as the lack of dates. I had no qualms about being single. I was confident I could find a date when I wanted one, but the fact that I hadn't really even looked to date lately, well that was concerning.

"I flirted with a few of my old high school classmates," I finally began. "I even briefly entertained the thought of making out with the former quarterback in his pickup truck, but my heart just wasn't in it."

"You didn't even give him a chance? You might've enjoyed it."

"Eh. By the time one AM rolled around, I was bored and my buzz was wearing off. I caught a ride home with an old classmate who was—no joke—pregnant, and therefore sober."

Stella laughed uproariously at my pathetic night out, then let me eat my lunch in peace for a few minutes before asking me about the rest of my weekend.

"It was pretty lame. On Thanksgiving, I slept in then helped my mom cook. Then the extended family came over for the meal."

There was nothing extraordinary about this Thanksgiving versus every other Thanksgiving. My grandparents, aunts, uncles, and cousins all arrived by mid-afternoon, and they all sought to pester me about current boyfriends or the lack thereof. They spent the night, and then all the women in the family hit the black Friday sales in the morning while the guys set up the Christmas tree and strung out the outdoor lights. We ordered pizza Friday night, went to a matinee Saturday, and by Saturday night, my cousins headed back home. My grandparents left Sunday morning after brunch, leaving me alone to pack.

I actually liked all the family time, and the break from school couldn't have been better timed, but I had started to go a little crazy with all the quiet. Well, 'quiet' wasn't the right word. My brothers were obscenely loud, from the moment they woke, until the second they finally powered down their gaming system.

But without more to stress about or more need to interact, my mind kept drifting. I couldn't stop thinking about boys, and why there wasn't one I really liked this semester. My mother wasn't helping matters any with her interrogations. Whereas most parents were quizzing their daughters about grades and their readiness for final exams, my mom expressed concern over my lack of boyfriend not once, not twice, but five separate times in three days. The most offensive occasion was when I was trying on a dress that turned out to be a bit too tight and she suggested that perhaps I was using food to replace a man in my life. It was a size 4, for crying out loud.

"A bunch of guys I went to high school with are hot now," Stella said, interrupting my daydream.

"Well, none of the guys I graduated with suddenly blossomed into hunks. They all just seemed really immature," I said.

Honestly though, all the guys at college struck me as immature, too. If I wanted to hang out with guys obsessed with video games, sports, and models, I'd just spend time with my brothers. I had no interest in dating someone like that. They only guy I even knew who didn't act like a teenager was Owen.

Stella made a pouty face, then started suggesting guys at school I could date. My mind wandered further.

I wasn't naïve enough to think I'd ever be anything more than a student to Owen, but that didn't stop me from fantasizing. He was everything I wanted in a man right now.

Obviously, he was good looking, but he was also mature. He was smart, polite, and gainfully employed. I strongly suspected he hadn't wasted his entire break playing Fortnight.

"Well, sorry you didn't have more excitement over break," Stella finally said, wadding up the deli paper holding her bagel. "Maybe you got the therapeutic rest time you needed though."

I hoped she was right. This morning, everyone on campus was still wound up from traveling, turkey, and shopping, but I knew the mood would become somber in a matter of days as students hunkered down for final exam prep. I wasn't too stressed about my finals yet, but I knew I'd have to work out a study plan at some point. Still, maybe the break from the social scene would prove beneficial to me.

The next day, I was slowly packing up my backpack after Italian, debating whether I should stick around and chat with Owen, when he motioned for me to approach his desk.

Flattered, I tried to hide my smile as I glanced around to see if any of my classmates were still around. Somehow, they'd already all exited the classroom. Not that I needed their validation to feel good as the teacher's pet, but it wouldn't hurt either. Years of being written off as a dumb blonde had taken a toll on my academic ego.

"What's on your schedule for next semester?" Owen asked.

I listed my upcoming course load as I wedged my notebook into my backpack, careful not to bend the already-frayed corners of my novels.

Owen frowned. "No Italian?"

I winced. "Sorry."

"Why not? You're a natural."

"It was just something I tried for fun. I don't need it for my degree."

31

"You can't tell me you didn't enjoy learning Italian. And I thought you still needed to choose a minor."

I zipped my backpack. "Honestly, if I was just now doing my schedule, I would continue it. I'm not excited about that linguistics course and would drop it in a heartbeat, but it's too late to add Italian for next semester."

Owen leaned closer. "Not if you know the professor."

I glanced up at him. He grinned widely and winked.

"Are you saying you got the job? Here?" I was already excited for him, but wanted confirmation that I wasn't misinterpreting before I started jumping up and down. I knew that was the exact position he wanted, but he'd been so down on his chances that I hadn't considered it really happening.

He nodded.

"Oh my God, that's amazing! Congratulations!" I hugged him tightly, and before I knew what was happening, my lips were on his.

The more I replayed the mortifying moment later, the less certain I became of my initial conclusion, which was that he kissed me back.

We broke apart almost as quickly as we'd come together, and I immediately averted my gaze to the ground, wishing a hole would appear and swallow me up.

"I'm so sorry," I mumbled.

"No, I, uh," Owen stammered, then cleared his throat. "I should go." He turned and left before I got the nerve to glance up.

* * *

THREE DAYS LATER, there was an email from Owen Chambers. Before I even opened it, my heart raced and my cheeks blushed, although I was alone in my room. It was short and direct.

> Dear Bridget-
>
> I took the liberty of checking your spring schedule and added you to my Tues/Thurs 10:15-11:30 am Italian 300 class. You have until January 15 to drop your linguistics class without penalty, or if you prefer, I'll remove you from this class. However, I think this course would be an excellent addition to your studies and suspect you would truly enjoy a minor in Italian. And from a selfish standpoint, I wouldn't mind having a familiar face or two in my first class as an Associate Professor. I'll see you at our Creole exam Thursday.
>
> Buona fortuna!
>
> Respectfully,
>
> Owen Chambers

I REREAD the email several times before deciding I was either reading too much into it, or not enough. I called down the hall for Stella, who immediately came in.

"Can you read this email?"

She nodded, read it over my shoulder, then shrugged. "Okay."

"It's from my Italian teacher, you know, the one who is in one of my French classes with me."

"The cute one?"

"Is he cute?" I asked, feeling myself blush more.

Stella laughed. "From the way you've described him, very. Plus he speaks two romance languages. That's sexy."

I shook my head, trying to stay focused, but thankful I hadn't told her about the kiss incident. "Is there something strange about his email?"

She reread it, then shook her head. "No. He sounds like a nice guy. I'd take his class if I didn't suck at languages."

"And you don't think it would be weird, having him as a professor after being in a study group with him?"

Stella shrugged again. "You're in his class now, right? I don't think it's any weirder just because he's an actual professor. I'd take the class."

OWEN

The week before winter break, I drove over to the library to check out a few books to bring home with me. I was planning to spend a week in Chicago with a buddy and then drive back to my parents' house for Christmas Eve through the start of the new year. I didn't want to waste any time starting on my first article for publication as a professor, and I knew my hometown wouldn't have the books I needed for my research.

As I headed out of the library, I noticed a familiar face waiting at the bus stop. She glanced up right as I walked by.

"I didn't think professors needed to be at the library this week," Bridget said.

I smiled, certain I'd never get sick of being called a professor. "Just picking up some books for break. How are finals going?"

"You tell me. You're the one with the gradebook," she quipped, tossing her hair over her shoulder.

I chuckled, certain she knew she'd done well on my exam. "How many more do you have?"

"Just one, and it's the spoken exam for my French conversation class. And I still have to finish the final paper for Creole."

I didn't think she'd appreciate hearing that I had churned out that essay over a week ago, with final exam time actually being pretty light for professors. So, I simply nodded. Then, I glanced around, seeing no buses in sight.

"Where are you headed?" I asked.

"Well, I was planning to go pick up dinner for my friend Stella and me and then head back to the sorority, but the bus schedule is wacky this week so I might just walk back to the sorority."

I hesitated, then against my better judgment, spoke. "Come on, I'll give you a ride."

"You sure?"

I nodded and motioned for her to follow me to my car. Neither of us had mentioned her overzealous response to my job announcement since it happened, but I was still struggling to put it completely behind me. I wanted to be certain that it was unintentional, but my desire to know for sure wasn't strong enough to overcome my anxiety about discussing it ever again.

I dumped my books into the back of the car as Bridget climbed in and dropped her backpack on her lap. I had just started the ignition when her phone chimed.

"Figures," she mumbled. "Stella just bailed on me for chicken wings with a Sig Ep."

I couldn't discern if there was any particular significance to that particular fraternity, so I focused on the fact that she was now free for dinner.

"I was going to pick up something for myself anyway, so it's no problem. Where do you want to go?"

She gazed over at me uncertainly. "Um, wherever."

"Where were you planning to go?"

"The deli. Stella and I always get their Thai chicken salads when it's pasta night at the sorority." She wrinkled her nose. "Spaghetti made in bulk for a hundred girls isn't their most appetizing meal."

"The deli works for me," I said, turning that direction.

Apparently we weren't the only people who had that idea, because parking was a nightmare. We ended up on a side street a couple blocks away. It was unseasonably warm for December though, so I didn't mind the walk.

We placed our orders to go, but by the time our food was ready, the sky had exploded with a torrential downpour.

"This weather is insane," I said, checking the weather app on my phone. "Looks like it should pass quickly. Do you want to just eat here while we wait?"

"Sure." She grabbed napkins and then headed over to a table.

As we sat, I remembered something I'd meant to ask her about earlier but kept forgetting, in my excitement about the job.

"So listen," I began. "I know you said you dismissed the idea of spending fall semester in France, but have you considered the possibility of a shorter study abroad trip?"

Bridget raised an eyebrow. "Do you have something specific in mind?"

"There's a month-long intensive study course in Florence this summer. It'd give you credit hours towards your minor in Italian, plus you'd still have time to travel to France if you wanted."

She didn't answer, and I realized it was probably overstepping for me to even suggest the program. I'd already been pushy enough by registering her for another Italian class. I told myself I just wanted to ensure she reached her potential as a gifted Italian student, but...

"I won't be offended if you're not interested," I quickly added. "And if you need to work over the summer I guess it wouldn't work."

Bridget shook her head. "No, it sounds...intriguing. Maybe, um, email me the information on the program and I'll look over it."

We talked about our respective plans for winter break and then fast forwarded to our schedules for the spring semester. By the time we'd both finished eating, the rain had slowed.

"I should've brought an umbrella," I said.

Bridget shrugged. "Who would've thought it would rain tonight, though?"

"I can go get the car and pick you up so you stay dry," I offered.

She shook her head. "I won't melt. Besides, it's nearly stopped anyway."

We braced ourselves, then stepped outside. We made it to the end of the street, then there was a deafening crack of thunder

Bridget shrieked, and within an instant, we were inundated with the hardest rain I'd ever experienced. I was trying to walk quickly, but there were so many comically large puddles already that it was impossible to dodge them all at any pace faster than a walk. The raindrops were massive and relentless, pelting us without pause and seemingly from all angles. It was blinding, and cold.

We had almost reached the car when I heard a yelp. I turned and saw that Bridget had stepped in one such puddle and slid sideways. The left side of her jeans was soaked.

I winced as I lunged to help her up. Of all the women to slip in a puddle, Bridget would hate it the most. There was no way her designer clothes were intended to withstand errant rainstorms.

Our hands were both slippery from the moisture, so when I grabbed her hand the first time, I lost my grip and we both stumbled back. I reached again, this time clutching her elbow and carefully hoisting her to her feet. I motioned for her to hurry, somehow convinced I could still spare her from being completely drenched. She shook her head and pointed to her shoe, which had fallen partially off in the puddle.

I waited while she fumbled with her shoe, regretting ever offering to drive her since now she was certain to hate me. I braced myself for the anger, but when Bridget glanced up at me, she was smiling.

"What?" I shouted to be heard over the drumming of the rain.

Bridget only shook her head and giggled. Then, she turned her head up to the sky, facing the offending precipitation head on. After a moment, she turned back to me, still laughing.

I reached for her hand to guide her to the car, but we took it slowly now. We couldn't possibly get any wetter than we already were anyway. Just as we neared the car, the rain stopped. It didn't slow gradually, but rather happened instantaneously, almost as though it was all being pulled back up into the clouds.

I stared up to the heavens, flabbergasted.

Bridget looked at me, and I opened my mouth to start apologizing. If we'd only gotten the food to go like we'd planned, or even if we'd just waited another two minutes...

But before I said anything, she was laughing uncontrollably again.

"I don't think I've ever been this soaked outside the shower!" she shrieked in between giggles.

She reached up to her hair and slowly squeezed it, ringing out more than a full cup of liquid. "I think there's even more water inside my socks," she said.

I laughed too, realizing the complete absurdity of it all. I unlocked my car, praying I had a large towel, but all I found was a tiny rag the size of a washcloth.

I offered it to Bridget and she began laughing harder. "What am I going to do with that?"

She had a point. It could barely dry her hands, let alone anything else.

"I'm so sorry," I said, shaking my head. "You would've been better off with the bus."

"Where's the fun in that?" she asked. She leaned against the car, removing her shoes one at a time and emptying the water from them.

Still too discombobulated from her unexpected reaction to speak, I watched her. I was stricken with how beautiful she was, even soaking wet. Her hair hung limply against her back and was darker from the moisture. Her coat and jeans clung tightly to her, and her face had a dewy sparkle. Large droplets of water still trickled down her cheeks.

I stepped closer and reached towards her with the rag, gently blotting the water off her face. Her bold green eyes caught my attention, and I couldn't look away. Everything about her was captivating, and in that moment, I forgot who we were, where we were, and how sopping wet we were. Every ounce of my attention was focused on this gorgeous woman who laughed at the rain. Never before had I been surprised so much and so often by another person.

Bridget's hand rose and covered mine. Whether she meant to stop me or help me, I didn't know, because she didn't move it further. She just rested it there over mine as we stared at each other. My skin tingled at her touch, a jolt of energy shooting straight down my torso. I imagined this was how a magnet felt, powerlessly pulled towards another lodestone.

A moment later, a loud clap of thunder exploded above and we jumped apart. The rag fell to the ground, so I bent to pick it up, tossing it onto the floor of the backseat.

"It's going to ruin your car seat if I get in," Bridget said, wincing at her drenched pants.

I smiled. "I'm not much better. Come on. You'll get pneumonia if you're out much longer."

We were both quiet the rest of the short drive. Bridget apologized again for soaking my car and thanked me for the ride, and I wished her good luck with her paper and oral exam.

She didn't hesitate hopping out as we neared her sorority, but then she did lean back in before walking off. "I guess I'll see you after break, Professor. Merry Christmas!"

"You too," I said, but she'd already scampered off.

CHAPTER 5

OWEN

*A*fter not seeing Bridget for a full month, I wasn't sure what to expect when I returned to campus. I couldn't deny we'd shared a moment, that something had passed between us that rainy night. But maybe that was all just the culmination of a tense semester. I'd presented my thesis, earned my dream job, and all along, Bridget was right there.

Between the brief kiss earlier and the way she looked at me in the rain, though, I couldn't help but suspect I wasn't the only one dwelling on what was happening between us.

I actually had myself convinced I wouldn't be attracted to her anymore. It wasn't like I'd pined for her over break. My buddy Scott and I had hit the town every night I was in Chicago, and I had enjoyed the company of several ladies that week. I hadn't actually slept with any of them, but really, I just wasn't the one-night-stand type of guy anymore. Besides, now that I was an actual tenure-track Associate

Professor, I was determined to possess the maturity expected of such a position.

Unfortunately, I was wrong. The second I heard Bridget's voice, laughing and talking with some guy in the hall outside the classroom, my pulse increased. Then, she waltzed in, wearing skintight jeans, a long cream-colored sweater, and tan boots that reached her knees, and I knew I was in trouble.

"Buongiorno Professore Chambers," she greeted as she sauntered past, smiling widely. She swung her long, now brown hair behind her back. I wondered what had inspired the color change, but thankfully knew well enough not to ask.

I smiled politely at her and the rest of the group following her in and then began class. I planned to hurry out of the classroom the moment class ended so as to avoid any solo conversation with her, but as it turned out, my panic was unwarranted. She walked out with a classmate named Jack, then paused at the entrance to the room and held up her palm, waiting patiently while he scribbled something.

Relief washed over me. The last thing I needed this semester was to be hung up on a student. But if I couldn't stop thinking about how gorgeous she looked, it wouldn't matter if she remained totally indifferent to me.

During our second class, Bridget was similarly aloof. But after class the following Tuesday, when I was alone in the classroom, trying to finish grading the last two papers in the stack I'd started before class ended, Bridget popped back in. She had been one of the first students out, so it startled me when she scurried back in, immediately flattening her back against the wall beside the door.

I eyed her with alarm. "Everything okay?"

She nodded but didn't move.

I waited for her to say something, but when it was clear

she wasn't going to, I pressed for more answers. "Are you hiding from someone?"

Another nod.

I frowned and rose to my feet. "Are you in danger?"

Now she shook her head, her cheeks flushed. She waited another moment, then stepped forward. "Sorry. I'll get out of your hair now."

I stepped forward. "Bridget, wait. If there's someone out there that..." my voice trailed off as I had no clue exactly what she was avoiding. "Why don't you sit down and tell me what's going on?"

She appeared to consider this, then slowly walked to a seat in the front row. I abandoned my papers at the desk and took the seat beside her.

"It's not like a serial killer or anything," she explained, her cheeks flushed, "just someone I'd rather not see. My ex."

"Oh. Is this a recent ex?" I asked, cringing as soon as the words left my mouth.

"No," she said, not appearing even slightly phased by my inappropriate and nosy question. "I mean, we sort of hung out again over winter break. Fucking ski trip," she mumbled, shaking her head. "I just...can't...deal with him today. Or ideally, ever again. It turns out Stella is right and I only date assholes. Is that possible? To have my type be jerks? It's not even like a bad boy thing. Just mean guys apparently."

I had no idea how to respond to any of this, but thankfully she was just staring at her sequined, magenta-colored nails while rambling on. I zoned out for a moment, trying to remember if there was another class scheduled in this room soon.

"And my hair color? None of his business. My hair, my choice. That seems like a pretty basic thing, right? And no, my hair color doesn't dictate my mood. Who even says shit like that?"

"I think your hair looks nice," I interrupted, again instantly regretting my inability to stay quiet.

"Thank you," she said.

She blew out a sigh. "It's genetic, really. My predisposition to have bad taste in men. My mom loved Patrick. He's my ex. Of course, since we broke up she keeps saying I just need to find a major league baseball player to marry. I mean what kind of motherly advice is that? How am I supposed to meet a major league player anyway? It's not like they're attending college or setting up profiles on Match.com."

"I'm sorry, but why does your mom think you should marry a major league baseball player?"

Bridget sighed, as though it were obvious. "Because I love the Cubs. And she thinks I need a man with a hefty paycheck but not a career that will bore me to tears whenever he talks about it."

I frowned, finding so much to take issue with in that explanation.

"The only decent baseball player I even know is Jack. And I hardly think he's major league material, do you?"

"Jack? Like from my class?" I was flabbergasted. Was she actually asking me for dating advice? "I have no idea whether he's good enough to go to the major leagues."

Bridget paused, gazed up, then laughed. "I'm sorry. This has got to be the most ridiculous discussion a student has ever forced you into."

I shrugged. "It's alright. Beats grading papers."

She stood. "Well, I should let you get back to that. I need to hit up the bookstore before my next..." her voice trailed off as she glanced at the clock. "Crap."

"Can you go after class?" I asked, guessing the reason for her dismay.

She shook her head. "No, I have that stupid dinner meeting for French majors tonight and then the bookstore will be closed." She sighed. "I guess I'll catch up on the reading tomorrow night. Not sure how much architecture I can handle in one night though. Plus you know by tomorrow they'll just have the one super gross copy with old boogers and questionable stains on it," she said with another groan.

I raised an eyebrow, vaguely remembering her saying she was taking the medieval French architecture class with Professor Dumont. Judging from her tone, she didn't share my enthusiasm about the topic, but I couldn't imagine anyone not falling in love with that course.

"What's the name of the book? I took that class my first year as a graduate student and if it's still the same, you can borrow my copy for the semester."

Bridget pulled out her phone and held the screen up to me a moment later to show me the book list.

"Yep. I've got that. I can bring it to class Thursday," I began. "Except I guess you need it before then."

She shrugged. "Well, it's not the end of the world if…"

I shook my head. "No, I don't want you to get behind. I should be home later this evening, so if you just swing by after your department dinner meeting, you can pick it up then."

Bridget stared uncertainly. "From your office?"

"No, I'm in an apartment right off campus," I said, returning to my desk for a piece of paper where I could jot down the address. Then I froze, pen poised above the paper, realizing I'd just asked a student to my apartment at night. And not just any student, either. Bridget.

"Or actually I might have some work I could finish up at the office tonight if you'll be near the building for your meeting so you don't have to go out of your way," I said, quickly backpedaling.

"I have a car, so it's not a big deal. Besides, the campus

buildings creep me out after dark." She picked up the paper where I'd scrawled the address. "I really appreciate this."

She was out of the room before I could protest further.

BRIDGET

It was after eight o'clock when I pulled up in front of Owen's apartment building. My dinner meeting had ended just before 7:30, but I'd driven around for a bit, trying to calm down. Ever since that day in the rain, I'd successfully avoided Owen. Well, I avoided him to the extent possible considering that my GPA involved compulsory attendance in his class.

Of course, trying to avoid Owen had seriously backfired. If I hadn't been so determined to get my mind off of Owen over Christmas break, I wouldn't have so much as glanced at Patrick, let alone nearly hooked up with him before totally freaking out and dashing out of his hotel room topless. I shuddered just thinking about it.

The entire time I'd dated Patrick, he'd never once looked at me the way Owen did right as the rain stopped. Actually, no one had ever before looked at me like that. And probably no one ever would again.

Except Owen was my professor and so surely I was misinterpreting the look and even if I wasn't, it didn't matter because, well, Professor. It was maddening, really. There were still over a dozen cute guys my own age on the list of potential boyfriends Stella and I had started freshman year. Not to be arrogant, but I was confident most of them would go out with me if I asked, and with them, I'd be able to gauge if they were interested.

So why was I crushing on the one I clearly couldn't have?

I glanced at the clock, aware that my pep talk was having the opposite effect of what I'd intended. I hated feeling neurotic almost as much as I hated feeling insecure. Both emotions were rather foreign to me but were pounding me like waves in a hurricane now. I killed the engine on the car, reapplied lipgloss, and smoothed my hand over my hair. I still wore the same gray slacks and slinky black top I'd had on the last time Owen saw me, so at least I didn't have to worry about that.

I stepped out of the car, chuckling as I thought how funny it would be if he'd left the book on his front porch. If I didn't even have to talk with him, to see him—in close, private proximity, then all this anxiety was for nothing.

But there was no book on the porch. No reason for me to avoid interacting with him.

I rang the bell, barely having time to lick my lips before he answered.

As the door swung open, my eyes centered on Owen's chest, in part because it was at eye level, but also because he had changed. He was no longer in the button down shirt and slacks he sported when teaching. Now he wore jeans and a dark gray undershirt that clung to his muscles. He smelled of a woodsy aftershave, and as I glanced upwards I realized he'd shaved and likely showered since I saw him last.

I sucked my bottom lip between my teeth.

"Come in," he said casually.

I took the slightest step into his apartment. It was generally clean and grown up looking, but I couldn't take my eyes off of Owen long enough to thoroughly snoop.

He retrieved a large book off the coffee table and carried it over. "I started flipping through it again after I got it out," he said. "I know you're not thrilled about this class, but I guarantee it's fascinating."

I accepted the book and smiled. "Well, thank you, really. And um, about earlier," I swallowed loudly. "I'm sorry about that. I didn't mean to drag you into my girl drama."

He grinned. "Not a problem. Growing up with a twin sister I am fairly well versed in the world of girl drama."

I tried to think of a witty reply, even if only to cover up the sound of the pounding of my heart, but failed to focus on a single coherent thought. Why did he have to be so hot? It was really distracting. The department should've factored that in before hiring him.

"Bridget?"

I glanced up, realizing he was speaking.

"I know it's not my place to comment, but I really doubt you're destined to have bad taste in men till the end of time. You deserve a nice guy though, and I've seen you enough to say that you know the difference between the good guys and the jerks. You just have to remember what you're worth."

"What I'm worth," I repeated, confused.

Owen opened and closed his mouth several times before finally speaking. His piercing blue eyes didn't leave mine the entire time.

"You're smart and kind and beautiful. I'm sure you could marry a major league baseball player if you wanted, but you could do so much more," he said.

I was loosely aware that my breathing had increased and my fingers and toes were going all tingly and numb. But I couldn't look away.

"Owen, I…" I had no clue where I was headed with that sentence, but when I gave up trying to figure it out, I realized I'd reached for his hand.

Owen glanced down, appearing equally surprised that our fingers were now touching, and when he gazed back up at me, his eyes had darkened.

He leaned in slowly, or at least it felt that way. The moment between me realizing my dream was about to come true and our lips actually making contact stretched for an eternity. When his mouth finally reached mine, I felt my entire body relax, as though all this tension had built up just for one, soft kiss. Except the kiss didn't stay soft for long. I'd barely begun to savor my first true taste of his lips pressed gently against mine when the kiss changed, deepening.

In an instant, my back was pressed against the door and Owen's full, hard frame leaned against me, sparking a plethora of sensations throughout my entire body. His hands were on my cheeks, then in my hair, and I realized that my own fingers were digging into his back and inching lower towards his butt. It was the sort of kiss that made me feel like I was going to pass out from overstimulation, and it was fabulous.

Suddenly, Owen broke away from my mouth, leaving my lips tingling and cool. He turned his head to the side, but his body still pressed against mine and his arm remained beside my head as his hand leaned against the door.

"Bridget, I'm sorry," he mumbled. "I'm so sorry. I just..." His voice was deep and breathy, which only made me crave him more.

I tightened my hand against his back, urging him to resume the best kiss of my life.

"We can't," he whispered. "I'm your teacher."

"I don't care," I replied quickly. I noted that, while he had stopped the kiss, Owen hadn't actually pulled away from me. His breath still fell in quick, warm spurts on my cheek. That had to mean something.

"If anyone found out, they might think..." he began. "It could jeopardize your degree."

"I don't care," I repeated. I started to initiate another kiss, then hesitated. I hadn't reviewed the university policies on the topic, but I assumed Owen had way more to lose than I did from our relationship turning physical. "Unless you don't want to," I added finally, gazing up at him for confirmation.

Owen shut his eyes tightly. Neither of us spoke for a

moment. "You even smell amazing," he said.

"I should go," I said, aware that he was trying to distance himself from me. "I don't want to mess things up for you."

I ducked under his arm, reaching down for the book I hadn't even realized I'd dropped.

"You should go," he agreed. "But I sure don't want you to."

I turned to stare at him. Even as his crystal blue eyes pleaded with me, I could sense the conflict within him from the tiny, almost imperceptible movements in his face.

"I don't want to go either," I whispered.

"Bridget, I've wanted you since the moment I laid eyes on you. When I saw you in French class that first day, you were a dream come true," he laughed weakly. "But since I knew you were in my Italian class, and an undergrad, my student, well I thought the universe was playing a cruel joke on me."

He stepped closer and reached for my hand. "I had to get to know you. I wanted to be close to you and I thought that would be enough, but I…" He exhaled slowly. "I need you to understand that the best thing for you would be for you to leave now. But if you're asking what I want, I want you to stay."

My throat felt dry but the rest of my body sprung to life more with each word he spoke.

"I won't hold it against you if you leave, Bridget, and I…"

I pushed my lips against him before he could talk me out of it.

Owen hesitated for a few seconds, then fully engulfed my lips with his own. The kiss immediately ricocheted back to the intensity level where we'd left off, but this time, our hands were moving more vigorously. He swiveled us around so his own back was against the door and he slipped my shirt up over my head. The second my shirt hit the floor, he focused his lips on my neck.

I fumbled for the hem of his shirt and thrust my hands

up, stifling a moan as my fingers grazed the ridges of his abdomen. I felt Owen tug at the button to my pants and a moment later, I was stepping out of them. I became aware of how unequal our states of undress had become and set about to remedy the situation, pulling his shirt upward. He took over the task for me, quickly shrugging out of his shirt then pausing, his gaze locked on my nearly nude body. His eyes widened happily and I flushed with pride at the realization that this unbearably sexy man found me attractive.

Things progressed quickly from there, with Owen's pants dropping to the floor before I fully realized I'd unfastened them and my bra slipping down my arms. By the time Owen picked me up, nudging my legs around his waist, we were both down to our underwear. He carried me to his bedroom, depositing me onto the plush gray comforter and collapsing on top of me, barely breaking the kiss.

I squirmed against him, forcing his hardened length to rub against me right where I desperately craved the friction. He took the hint and pressed against me for a moment, slipping his hand down to my breast. As his fingers touched my nipple, an immensely pleasurable electrical current shot through my body and I dizzily realized I couldn't wait much longer to have him inside me. I reached down for the waistband of his boxer briefs, but could only slide them down an inch or so. He gazed at me, a mischievous grin on his face, then crept down my body, his mouth focusing on each breast before heading to its ultimate destination.

His tongue lapped along the outside of my thin panties and the pressure building within my core mounted. He repeated the gesture, and I moaned, unable to contain my cries of pleasure any longer. Owen gazed up at me as he worked my last remaining article of clothing over my thighs and down my legs, pausing tauntingly before diving back towards me with his mouth.

His left hand reached for my breast as his tongue teased my clit, and that was all it took for me to shatter around him. The exquisite spasms pulsing throughout my body were like nothing I'd ever experienced before. But every sensation felt so good that I greedily craved more.

I nudged Owen back up my body and kissed him breathlessly until I stopped seeing flashes of light behind my eyelids. Then I pushed up to my elbows, eager to finish what we'd started. Despite my intense release, my body was still tightly wound and yearning for more. I tugged his boxer briefs down, moaning happily when my hands reached his firm, bare ass that felt every bit as good as I'd imagined.

Owen pulled away and reached into his nightstand.

I paused, confused, then realized what he was doing when I heard the rip of the foil packet. He caught me staring and nipped my breast, eliciting another wanton cry from my lips. He rolled the condom down his length then kissed me hard on the mouth.

"Are you sure?" he whispered, his lips grazing my ear.

I nodded, then practically purred, "Yes. God, yes." But really it wasn't a fair question because his fingers had already begun stroking my wet folds and I couldn't have said no even if I'd wanted to at that point. I was too breathless and too dizzy and all of my faculties were focused solely on the inundation of pleasurable physical sensation taking place all over my body.

His mouth found mine again and just as I decided he was the best kisser alive, he reached my entrance and pressed forward. I gasped at the sudden intrusion and his hips froze. He focused all his efforts on my breasts for a moment, his mouth lavishing them with all the attention my lips had been receiving. When he returned his tongue to mine, my body had eagerly stretched to accommodate him and I lifted my hips to meet him thrust for thrust.

I must have been subconsciously aware that this would be my only chance to be with Owen like this, because I was determined to hold out longer. My body threatened to reach orgasm almost immediately, but I wanted more. More time, more build up, more of this deliciously tantalizing fullness as he slid out then angled back in, hitting the exact right spot with each thrust.

I wrapped my legs around Owen's back, allowing him to reach even deeper. Finally, as his hand reached back towards my hardened nipples, I couldn't resist any longer. My skin was on fire and every cell in my body imploded at the same time, filling me with wave after wave of pleasure. Owen picked up the rhythm of his hips and I sensed his body tightening above me right before he slammed into me one final time, moaning loudly.

We both lay still for several minutes trying to catch our breath. Actually, I may have literally blacked out for a moment since I have no memory of him pulling out of me, removing the condom, or pulling the covers over us. By the time my pulse had returned to a somewhat stable rhythm though, the panic and realization of what I had done began to wash over me.

I started to scoot out of the bed.

"Stay," he commanded.

My face must have revealed my surprise, because he quickly explained.

"I know we can't do this again. But for now, you're here. I don't want it to be over yet," he said softly, tracing his finger along the length of my now dark hair.

I hesitated, then let him draw me closer. I listened to the calming rhythm of his pulse through his chest and tried to mimic his steady breathing, but I must have failed, because he abruptly pulled away and stared at me, alarmed.

"You aren't a, er, weren't..." he sighed, "I mean, that wasn't your first time..."

"Oh," I said, as soon as I figured out what he was asking. "No." I considered offering more explanation, but decided we weren't really at that point.

"Are you sure?"

I couldn't help but laugh. How could I not be sure? "Yes," I said. "I had a steady boyfriend freshman year. My ex, Patrick. We broke up last spring."

Owen was silent for a moment. "Sorry. It's just, well, you're shaking."

"Do virgins shake?"

He breathed a laugh. "I don't know. I wanted to make sure you were okay, I guess." He paused. "Are you? Okay?"

The truth was I didn't know. I felt such a mixture of emotions at that moment that it was hard to sort out any of it. "I think I'm cold and maybe a little anxious."

He pulled me closer and pulled the blanket up over us. "I've never heard of being anxious afterwards."

"I didn't exactly have a chance to be anxious before. It wasn't like I planned on sleeping with you when I came over tonight."

"I'm sorry," he said softly.

"Not planning it isn't the same as not wanting it," I said. "I've thought about doing that with you since October."

Owen grinned. "Really?"

"I couldn't exactly flirt with you."

"You kissed me."

I blushed. "You remember that?"

He propped himself on his elbow. "Of course I remember. It was the best part of my week."

"You got your dream job that week," I reminded him.

"I know." He smiled at me. "I felt horrible afterwards

though. I figured I was flirting too strongly with you and that's why you did it."

"I felt like a fool."

"You're not a fool."

"I kissed a teacher."

"I slept with a student," he retorted.

"Touché." I felt myself relaxing more. "Wait, am I the student?"

He groaned. "Yes! Do you think I go around seducing all the girls on campus?"

I shrugged playfully. "You have to know you're the hottest professor."

He shook his head and then we were quiet again. "This is wrong. So why does it feel…"

"Right?"

Owen sighed and we both grew quiet, drifting off to sleep.

When I awoke, my mind registered the weight of an arm draped around my waist and the warmth of a body pressed against my back, but it took me a moment to remember where I was. As soon as the full realization hit me, my body tingled with excitement.

I have Owen Chambers wrapped around my body, I thought dreamily. Of all the crushes I'd ever had, this was the one I least expected to materialize into anything real. I hadn't forgotten his words, that we couldn't do this again, and I knew he was right. But for now, I was here. With him.

I embraced the sensation of his chest expanding softly against me with each calming breath he took, inhaled the fresh, sporty scent of his aftershave, and smiled as his warm breath tickled my neck with each exhale. I relished every fleeting moment, knowing it wouldn't last much longer, and it didn't. He stirred, squeezed my body tighter to him, then kissed the back of my hair before releasing me.

How long had he been awake, I wondered, but it didn't matter. He was awake, and we both knew I couldn't stay the night. I sat slowly, and he followed suit.

"I should go," I said.

Owen nodded in agreement, but his eyes filled with regret.

He glanced down at his feet in the bed while I dressed, presumably to give me privacy, a courtesy I both appreciated and found ironic. He slipped into his boxer briefs and stood, delicately brushing a strand of hair off my face.

"I wish I'd met you under different circumstances," he said.

There was no great response for that, so I just smiled. He walked me to the door. He glanced out the peephole, then turned back to me.

"I'll watch you from the window to make sure you get to your car safely," he said apologetically.

I realized why he didn't want to risk being seen walking me to my car and frankly, I didn't feel his apprehension about my safety in the small college town was warranted, even this late at night. I paused, knowing so much was still unsaid between us.

"Owen, I don't regret what we did," I told him, my voice sounding more like a whisper. "But I understand why it can't happen again. You don't need to worry about me. I'm an adult, and we can both be mature about this." I nodded awkwardly. "I'll see you Thursday."

He frowned, then his face lit up with the probable realization that Thursday was the next time he would see me in class, as my professor. Owen reached for my hand and tugged, pulling me back to him.

I squealed at the suddenness of it, but fully lost myself to him as he enveloped my mouth in his with one last, fierce kiss.

CHAPTER 6

OWEN

I slept fitfully that night, tossing and turning until two hours before my alarm was set to go off and then sleeping like the dead until its shrill beeping startled me back to life. I rolled over and groaned, certain I could still smell her fruity perfume or lotion or whatever it was that smelled so damn good on my sheets. I inhaled sharply a few extra times before forcing myself out of bed.

I had two classes in the morning, then office hours followed by a department meeting in the afternoon. I had never before been so grateful for a busy day. I knew the second I had a break to catch my breath, my mind would wander. That would be bad. I checked my phone compulsively throughout the day, I suppose, in case Bridget called or texted. Except I knew that was ridiculous because she didn't even have my number. I probably had her number somewhere in her file because, as her professor, I had that sort of basic contact information. But that didn't make it appropriate for me to call.

I stayed at my office researching for my next paper much longer than I needed to. When I got home, I lifted weights for nearly an hour before I decided I was exhausted enough to attempt sleep.

My sleep was choppy and disturbed, again, but this time, I gave up before the sun came up. I bundled up and headed outside for a run, desperate to burn off the nervous tension before I went to class and saw her again.

What had I done?

For as long as I could remember, I'd dreamed of teaching Italian. As a kid, I was thrilled at the notion of someone paying me to speak a cool language and encouraging me to travel the world. In college, I was eager to help inspire other kids to love the language and culture the way I did. By grad school, I was positive that foreign language classes were the key to world peace and a better global economy. I was certain without a doubt that my intentions going in to this profession were pure.

How had I sunk so low? How had I gone from that idealistic student to a stereotypical creep?

It seemed like a pretty basic rule. Don't seduce the students. Actually, no one had explicitly showed me the rule, but I was positive the school still had a strong policy prohibiting professors from engaging in sex with students.

I wasn't worried that Bridget would tell anyone, and I didn't see how anyone would find out, but the fact that I knew what we'd done—and that I'd done it knowing it was wrong—deeply bothered me. I was less than two weeks into my first semester as a professor and already I'd broken the cardinal rule. At this rate, I'd be blackmailing students and accepting bribes for better grades by spring break.

I pounded the pavement, hoping the repetition of one

foot, other foot, one foot, other foot would somehow dull my searing guilt, or at least knock some sense into me. By the end of five miles, my shins ached and I felt like I'd punished myself, whereas my usual runs felt like a reward.

The moment I stepped into the steamy shower though, my thoughts switched immediately to Bridget. As I washed my hair, I felt her fingers frantically grazing my scalp. As I soaped my torso, I vividly recalled her hands eagerly roaming my flesh. The memories were so fresh and so detailed, and I clung to each clear vision, desperate to relive the whole night. But right before my body reached the release it craved, I switched the faucet to cold. I didn't deserve that, not after what I did.

BRIDGET

I spent the entirety of Wednesday locked in my own mind, alternating between replaying scenes of the prior night and panicking about the certain awkwardness awaiting me in class Thursday. I managed to fuddle through my classes Wednesday and completed—without any understanding or actual learning—the homework I couldn't postpone till the weekend.

I struggled the most with my Italian assignment. It was easy, a few simple pages of verb conjugations and about thirty new vocabulary words, as well as a fill-in-the-blank style essay. Normally I could complete this task in fifteen minutes, committing the new words to memory with ease and completing the written work as fast as my hand could move. But today, every word had new meaning, and every aspect of the language reminded me of him.

I went to the restroom on my way to his class the next afternoon, hiding out in the stall in hopes of steadying my pulse, but it was futile. The longer I waited, the more anxious

I became. I marched into the classroom, head down, and took my seat. When I did look up, I saw the classroom was nearly full, and Owen was facing away, deep in conversation with another student. I exhaled with relief, retrieved my textbook, notepad, and pens from my backpack, and switched my cell phone to vibrate.

I glanced up just as Owen finished his discussion with my classmate. Our eyes met briefly, and right as I felt my face flush, he dropped the stack of papers he was holding. Two female students from the front row flew out of their seats to assist him with the simple pick-up, and he grinned at me, embarrassed. I smiled back, and relaxed.

He began class, reviewing the materials from the prior day before starting on the new material. Owen was a good teacher, in all respects. He was very energetic and captivating as a lecturer, and it was obvious he put a great deal of effort into his lesson plans. I attributed that in part to his newness as a professor, and his probationary status, but I suspected he would beat the odds and still be this passionate about his subject after decades of teaching jaded collegiates.

At thirty some students, the class wasn't large, and Owen already knew most of us by name. He stuck to surnames, though, a formality I found endearing and respectful. Owen called to several students at random to read their homework essays aloud, and all but one had completed the assignment, albeit to varying calibers of accuracy. Then he moved on to the new conjugations, picking different verbs from those in our homework, asking us to apply the same rules and patterns.

He called on a student, turning to write on the chalk-board as she answered, then repeated the process with another student. The patterns were easy, the verbs following a much simpler pattern than the French ones I'd studied for years. I watched Owen as he grinned at the class and turned to write each new word on the chalkboard. His back and shoulder muscles rippled beneath his pale blue shirt. He wasn't wearing a tie; he rarely did, I had observed, and the top two buttons of the shirt were undone. I wondered if that was intentional, or if he always wore his shirts like that and I just hadn't noticed before.

Suddenly, I realized all eyes were on me.

"Ms. Williams?" Owen said, his tone immediately alerting me to the fact that he had already said my name, and possibly asked me a question, at least once while I was distracted.

I nodded to indicate I was now paying attention.

He pointed to the board so I knew which word I was expected to conjugate, but my mind blanked. All I could think of was the French equivalent. I opened my mouth to answer, then closed it momentarily, shaking my head.

"I don't know," I mumbled.

He frowned, but called on the girl next to me instead. She happily completed the task.

I tried to stay focused the rest of the class, but knew my chances of being called out again were slim to none. I tuned in when Owen listed the assignment for the next class, then dutifully gathered my materials and began haphazardly cramming it back into my backpack. I made my way to the door, ready to file out with the rest of the class, when Owen stopped me.

"Ms. Williams, can I see you for a moment?"

I froze and turned slowly. There were two other students at his desk, so he motioned for me to wait. I nervously awaited my turn, both eager and terrified of being alone with him again. Owen was perched on the edge of his desk, appearing carefree and totally comfortable in his own skin.

I backed away, sitting at a desk in the front row to offer some privacy to my classmate discussing a grade with him. I watched him stand to point to one of the words on the board, then fully retreated into my own world again as the first student left and he began discussions with the second. I barely noticed the silence in the room until Owen stepped closer, sitting on the edge of his desk again.

I glanced up and realized we were alone. The classroom door was open, and Owen was studying me curiously.

"Thanks for waiting," he said when I made eye contact. "Are you okay today?"

I nodded.

He frowned, clearly not convinced. "It's not like you to miss an easy question like that."

Now I snapped into student mode. "I completed the assignment. I just couldn't think of the answer when you asked."

He stared back at me, expressionless.

"I'm allowed to miss one," I insisted, feeling defensive. "Other students don't know half the verbs you've taught."

"But you do, Bridget. You could conjugate that in your sleep." He paused. "You seemed distracted today. I just wanted to check in and see if..." he blushed and glanced at the open door. The halls were quieting down as students from other classrooms had all exited the building as well. "There's nothing else going on, right? You're okay?"

I analyzed his words before replying. "I'm fine, Owen. I mean, Professor Chambers. There's nothing wrong. I was just a little distracted by, you know, but it won't happen again."

He swallowed and stared at his feet for a long pause. I took the opportunity to watch him again, admiring the casual posture he maintained, somehow managing to look like a department store model as he leaned against his desk. Having seen him in jeans and a tee shirt, as well as significantly less than that, I knew firsthand that his body was every bit as perfect as it seemed in his professional attire. I was in awe that he could look so arousing in boring chocolate brown slacks and a button down.

"Bridg...Miss Williams, I just want you to know that if you're going to be distracted in my class, I can probably help arrange a transfer into a different class. I know the rules say you can't transfer this late, but I'm sure if..."

"That won't be necessary," I interrupted.

"You're a good student and you don't deserve to struggle in a class because of a bad professor."

"You're an amazing professor."

"I make bad choices."

I laughed. "Don't we all," I mumbled.

He forced a smile.

I stood up, determining our discussion had concluded. "I appreciate your concern, Professor, and you have correctly ascertained the cause of my distraction, but you don't need to worry. It was a one-time thing. I will be my normal over-achieving self again by Tuesday."

Owen sighed and ran his fingers through his already-unruly hair. My stomach clenched at the unintended sexiness of his simple gesture. *Crap*, I thought. It was going to be harder than I expected to push him out of my mind.

"How is Professor Dumont's class going?" he asked.

I smiled, knowing he lacked my disdain for her teaching methods. "I was dreading the class, honestly... I mean, how could medieval French architecture possibly be that interesting? But surprisingly it's been okay. The reading is a bit tedious, but her lectures are fascinating. And she seems to like me."

"How could she not?" he asked, walking me to the door. "Have a good weekend. Practice those verbs," he teased.

CHAPTER 7

BRIDGET

As promised, I pulled it together by Tuesday. I concentrated so hard on not thinking about Owen as he led class that I had a massive headache rivaling the worst hangover ever by the time class ended. Thursday was a little easier, until Owen reminded the class of his prior offer of extra credit for anyone attending the Italian festival that night. I knew Owen would be there, and I had planned to go, well, before. I debated skipping it in the name of maintaining my sanity, but then it occurred to me if my distractibility didn't improve ASAP, I might actually need the extra credit.

Besides, I'd already planned to carpool with a few friends from class. I didn't want to have to make up some lame excuse to justify my last minute change in plans. Erin had driven us, but Jack and Chris from our class came too. Out of the three of them, I knew Jack the best, but he had this annoying habit of flirting with me. Usually, I didn't mind it, and actually sort of enjoyed it, but tonight it was just irritating.

I told Erin I was going to go look for a sorority sister I thought would be there and that it was okay to leave without me if I wasn't back in a half hour. Realistically, I figured I'd find Owen, freak out about talking to him, and be back with Erin in under five minutes.

What actually happened was I wandered around, watching Owen from a distance, and then waved as soon as he turned my direction.

As Owen saw me, he nodded politely, his hands still in his pockets. Then he approached slowly.

"Where are your friends?"

"They left a little while ago."

"But you stayed?" He was still more than a healthy distance away, but even there I could still see his bold blue eyes piercing through the dim lighting.

I shrugged. He wasn't actually questioning whether I'd stayed, but why. I wasn't sure what the right answer was, so I went with honesty. "I wanted a chance to talk to you."

He glanced to the side, then down at his feet. "About?"

Nothing. Everything. I really didn't know. I took a deep breath, then exhaled, already missing the intensity of his stare.

"Did you drive?" he asked, frowning.

"No. But I can take a bus back to campus," I said, picking up on his unease.

Owen shuffled his feet nervously, then motioned for me to follow him. "I'll give you a ride," he said.

We walked to his car in silence. I stepped closer to him at one point, and he took two large, deliberate steps away. I couldn't tell if it was because we were in public or because he really didn't want anything to do with me anymore. I'd seen him staring at me earlier though. Of that, I was certain.

Every time Jack casually touched me, I turned to see Owen's gaze focused on me. Owen definitely felt something for me, but whether it was simply guilt and remorse or something more similar to what I felt, I didn't know.

The parking lot wasn't too crowded when we reached Owen's car, and I really saw no one notable when we left, but I reasoned that it actually wasn't too bad anyway for an associate professor to give a student a ride home. This wasn't high school, where teachers and students were really never supposed to be alone together outside of the classroom. Here, professors and students interacted much more outside of the lecture halls. I guessed there was just an expectation that we'd all respect the boundaries that were set.

He started the car, then hesitated before backing out of the space. He turned to me and my heart fluttered a little. I waited expectantly, praying he was going to kiss me or say something meaningful.

Owen cleared his throat. "Can you buckle?"

I glanced down, realizing I hadn't fastened my seatbelt. I chewed the inside of my cheek, disappointed that his only comment had been about my safety. As soon as my belt clicked into place, he pulled out of the lot. He was quiet, focused intently on the fairly empty roads. I snuck several glances at him, taking in his two-day stubble, his slightly mussed hair and the oh so masculine line of his jaw, framed perfectly by the fleeting lights from passing cars.

From this close, I could smell his cologne. I wondered if it was simply a lingering fragrance in his car, or if he'd worn it tonight. I yearned to press my face against his neck and inhale deeply. I held my breath, determined to maintain control. I was being ridiculous, I knew. I could have practically any guy I wanted on campus, at least for a night, I figured. So why did my body react so strongly to this particular guy?

"I can't focus with you staring at me," Owen said suddenly.

I turned abruptly towards my window. For a moment, I was still too focused on my memory of his perfectly carved abs and the sparse collection of dark blond hairs across his chest to take in my surroundings, but once I truly looked out the window, I realized we weren't headed towards my sorority.

"This isn't the way to the house," I said.

"I thought you wanted to talk," he replied.

I bit my lip. I had said that, but clearly what I wanted was to launch myself onto his lap and stroke every part of his body, first with my hands, then with my mouth... Damn it. What was wrong with me? I forced myself to count backwards from ten in French, then Italian, a random calming exercise I'd started as of late. When I reached "uno," I blurted out the first question that came to my mind.

"Why Italian?"

He glanced quickly at me, his face filled with confusion. Clearly that was not what he expected me to ask about. After a full minute of awkward silence, he answered, his voice cracking slightly. "My grandma, on my mom's side, is Italian. She's lived in the US since World War Two, but we still have some family there. I spent a summer in Palermo when I was ten and learned a good chunk of the language then."

"Oh, wow." I'd had no idea the language was so personal to him. "Do your parents speak Italian?"

"My mother is fluent but only speaks it with my grandmother. My father never really picked up much of the language."

I smiled, trying to picture Owen as a child. He would've been adorable, scampering about the Italian countryside with that mischievous grin and huge dimple.

"And you? Why Italian?"

I started with the explanation I gave everyone. "It's the same department as French and similar enough to be easy to learn. I'm terrible at math and science..."

"I doubt that," he interjected.

I ignored the interruption. "So it made sense to pad my schedule with more language arts classes." I paused. "I petitioned my high school to offer Italian classes. I wanted to learn it instead of French, actually."

Owen reached a gradual stop at a red light and turned to me. "Really?"

I nodded, turning quickly away. I couldn't lock eyes with him and not get lost in my own fantasies again. "They told me there wasn't enough interest to form a class, and that it didn't have as much real life application as French."

"That's true," he said. "But what sparked your interest in the first place?"

I fidgeted with my bracelet. "Shakespeare," I finally said.

"He was English, not Italian."

I felt my cheeks flush. "I know, but many of his characters weren't. So many of his plays were set in Italy, and I always dreamed of someday going to the places that inspired all of these gorgeous words."

Owen didn't answer, but his breathing was labored. I nervously turned towards him and saw his hands both firmly gripping the wheel, his chest rising noticeably with each breath. I watched his Adam's apple bob as he swallowed.

"What's wrong?"

"Nothing," Owen whispered.

"It's stupid, I know. But I just, well, I didn't enjoy a lot of classes in high school and when we started reading Shakespeare, I really connected to all the emotions in his writing. I'd lose myself in the fields of Verona and dream about the marketplace in Padua or the Venetian canals. I just..."

"It's not stupid," he interrupted.

I shrugged, not that he could see it. "Well, apparently it's unclear if Shakespeare ever even visited Italy, so who knows if his descriptions are even that accurate."

"You can go and see for yourself," he said.

"Yeah. Maybe someday." I twisted my finger around the hem of my shirt, desperately trying to keep my hands occupied so I wouldn't feel so acutely the absence of his skin against my own. I had thought a few minutes alone with Owen would make me feel better, but being this close to him without touching him was actually torture.

Suddenly, the car veered to the side. I had no sooner ascertained that we were now pulled along the side of a random street, devoid of other traffic at this hour, when Owen shifted the car into park.

He unfastened his belt and turned to me in one fluid motion, his mouth crashing into mine before I could even register what was happening. My heart raced but my fidgeting hands calmed instantly. The heat from his tongue was a sharp contrast to the frigid night air, and the urgency with which he devoured my lips caused a startling visceral response zipping throughout my body like an electrical current.

His hands reached for my face as mine went for his arms. I struggled to stifle a satisfied groan as my fingers squeezed the firm flesh of his biceps, which were every bit as exquisite as I remembered. One of us unbuckled my belt, enabling my other arm to reach for his thigh. I was consumed with the need to feel more of him, even as I felt myself gasping for breath amidst the passionate kiss.

I could've stayed like that forever, but at the fleeting flash of light from a passing car, the moment ended as quickly as it had begun. Owen pulled back, thrusting his hands into his hair.

"Fuck," he muttered under his breath.

I didn't say anything. I was literally too breathless to speak.

After a minute, I tentatively reached my hand back to his thigh. He stiffened at my touch, then clasped my hand in his own. He squeezed it encouragingly, then gently placed it back on my own lap. He reached over and fastened my belt around me, lingering by my ear.

"I'm sorry," he whispered. "We can't."

I understood immediately, but with my nerve endings all still tingling with excitement, I couldn't formulate any response.

Owen waited another minute, then carefully pulled back onto the road. He steered directly to my sorority, stopping on the corner. "I'll see you in class," he said, avoiding my stare.

I fumbled with my belt, shaking, then stood. "Thank you for the ride." I shut the door behind me and went straight into my room.

I grabbed my robe and shower caddy and headed into the bathroom, somehow managing to wait until the steamy water blasted into me to succumb to the sobs clamoring to exit my body.

I'd never felt that type of connection with a man before Owen, and I had certainly never been kissed like that before. Everything about him was perfect for me. The way he looked at me, the way he touched me, and oh God the way his tongue moved against mine...it was all absolute perfection.

I felt like it should've been easier this way, knowing our chemistry wasn't just in my head, but instead, the acute awareness that Owen Chambers was every bit as drawn to me as I was to him made the entire situation even more tragic. Now we were just another pair of star-crossed lovers, kept away by mere circumstance.

CHAPTER 8

OWEN

I made no effort to sleep that night, recognizing as soon as I returned home the futility of an attempt at rest. Instead, I dove into my research, pounding out another four pages on my article. Clearly, extreme sexual frustration was a blessing to my career success. If this tension continued, I'd be the most published professor before my third year.

I wished I could chalk it up to chemistry, because that, I suspected, would be tolerable. Bridget Williams was the sexiest, most gorgeous woman I'd ever laid eyes on. Her beauty wasn't solely in my eyes, either. I saw the way other guys on campus stared at her. Even the other women acted differently around her, some intimidated by her appearance and others clearly resentful. But I had been attracted to other beautiful women I couldn't claim as my own in the past, and it was manageable. This was not. This was different.

It was so much more than physical attraction, but I

couldn't explain how. Bridget was smart and sassy yet surprisingly sweet. She was confident but not cocky, and she was oh so much deeper than I could've imagined. Every time I spoke with Bridget I uncovered a new, fascinating layer to her that made her even more perfect. When she spoke about her love of Shakespeare fueling her interest in Italy, I swear I felt my heart skip a beat.

I'd always recognized myself as a hopeless romantic, not just in actual romantic relationships, but in all areas of life. I was a dreamer. I followed my heart, not my head, with many major decisions. Learning Bridget was not only the same way, but also similarly hid that truth about herself from the world at large, well, it physically affected me. I couldn't not kiss her then. I knew it was wrong before I'd even done it, but still, I couldn't truthfully say I regretted it. As hard as it was now, sitting alone in my apartment, the tantalizing scent of her hair still detectable on my fingers, I wasn't sure I could've endured another moment without kissing her.

I shut my laptop roughly, scooting it across my desk. I flipped to a new page in my yellow legal pad and began writing a note.

"Dear Bridget," I began.

I paused there, unsure of what else to say. She deserved more than a "sorry, not sorry, and don't look at me again with those puppy dog eyes" sort of note. Better to keep it simple. And, I realized, anonymous. I ripped out the page and tore it to shreds. An hour later, I finally had the finished note. It read:

I owe you an apology. I was wrong, all of it was wrong, and you deserve so much more. I can't say I regret any of it, and for that, I am sorry. But this has serious ramifications not just for me but for you too. We can't talk by phone, we can't text or email, and we definitely can't... I wish things were different.

When my morning alarm went off, I was still dissatisfied with the final draft, but it would have to do. I went for a brisk jog to wake me up, then took a hot shower while my coffee brewed.

I was on hyper-alert when my class was due to start. I wondered if Bridget would even show, debating whether it would be easier if she weren't there. Her presence would be distracting for sure, but her absence may be even more so.

I didn't have to wonder long. She was the fourth student to arrive. She glanced at me on her way in, then quickly averted her eyes. I powered through my class, avoiding looking at the entire section of the class seated near Bridget. With ten minutes left to go, I announced the homework assignment.

Then, I added, "I'm heading out of town for the weekend, so there will be no office hours today. I'm ending class a few minutes early though, so if anyone has questions for me, stick around and we will chat now." I paused to grab the stack of papers on my desk. "Stay in your seat until you've gotten your last test back. Overall you guys did well. We will review some of the trickier conjugations again next week."

I quickly distributed the graded papers, my hand shaking as I carefully handed Bridget hers. The note I'd written was inside a blank envelope between the first and second pages of her test. I made eye contact as I distributed her paper, hoping she'd look at it in class instead of dropping the envelope.

I proceeded to the next student, but glanced back just in time to see Bridget flip to the next page of her test, spot the envelope, then glance up at me conspiratorially. When the last test had been distributed and the students stood and began to disperse, I noticed Bridget lingering. Luckily, I shook my head slightly and she understood, nodding back before leaving.

As soon as the last student left, I hightailed it out of the building and off campus. I headed back home for the weekend, visiting with my parents a bit but spending the vast majority of my time with an old friend. Drinking beer while alternating playing pool, darts, video games, and basketball was as good of a distraction as any I could hope for.

By Monday morning when I returned to campus, I felt ready to face my students again—all of them.

What I wasn't prepared for, though, was for Bridget to completely ignore me our entire class Tuesday and then show up to my office hours. As always during office hours, I left my office door open. When I was meeting with a student, another faculty member, or taking a phone call, I'd shut the door. The aged vinyl blinds covering my window into the hallway were generally open, though, so I could generally tell when a student arrived and presumably, they could tell what I was doing as well. However, I still tried to open my door as soon as my meeting or call concluded.

I was ten minutes into a phone call with my faculty mentor, unaware that enough time had passed for it to actually be my office hours already, when I saw Bridget pass by the window. She wore floral leggings and a long, flowing top, and her hair was pulled into a tight bun on top of her head. She wore pink slipper-style shoes that accented the impression that she was a ballerina. I wondered whether she'd ever been a dancer, imagining her grace and beauty would've easily made her a star. I quickly averted my eyes, confused at how something that I normally remained oblivious to, like a woman's outfit, was so intriguing to me when it came to Bridget.

When my phone call ended, I knew I needed to open the door and begin my meetings. But I was terrified. What if she was still there, waiting to speak with me? What if she'd left? I took a slow, deep breath, then went to the door.

I casually glanced into the hallway, seeing only Bridget. This wasn't a surprise, as my office hours weren't normally jam-packed with students.

"Come in Ms. Williams," I said politely, standing back. She went into the small office but stood in a corner. "Take a seat." I gestured to the chairs on the opposite side of my desk then closed the door and walked around my desk, grateful for the large physical barrier between us.

She stared at me expectantly and I could tell she was nervous, but the longer she waited to speak, the more nervous I grew as well.

"Is this about your test?" I asked.

She shook her head.

"My note then?" I guessed.

"Where were you this weekend?" she asked.

"Back in my hometown. I needed to get away," I said.

She nodded, her perfectly shaped light brown eyebrows furrowing together.

"You read the note?"

She nodded again.

I wasn't sure what else to say.

"I don't agree," she blurted out.

I opened my mouth, then shut it again. I was confident at my precise memory of the note's wording, and I really didn't see any place for disagreement.

"I understand what you're saying. I don't want to get you in trouble. I can... I can handle not telling anyone and not emailing or calling. But I want to see you again."

"Bridget, we can't..."

"We are both adults. And if you aren't interested, that's different."

She looked straight at me and it was like her bright green eyes were piercing right into my soul.

"But I think you are," she continued, "I know you have

high standards of ethics and I think that we can keep our friendship out of the classroom entirely separate from what goes on in the classroom."

"You want...friendship," I repeated, forcing myself to breathe.

Bridget glanced out the window to the still-empty hallway before turning back to me. "I want you," she said finally. Her tone was light, but the implication wasn't.

It took all of the self-restraint I could muster to remain seated. My entire body buzzed with excitement that the woman I wanted more than I'd ever wanted anything or anyone my entire life sat before me telling me she wanted me in a way that I knew meant more than just friends.

And then my stomach lurched at the realization that this changed nothing.

I squeezed my eyes shut, grateful at least that she had remained seated and, to anyone looking in, probably appeared like any other student. I, on the other hand, probably looked like a serial killer trying to talk down one of my multiple personalities. My breath was coming hard and fast and I'd balled my hands into tight fists under my desk.

"We can't," I finally said. "There are rules."

When I garnered the courage to look at her, she nodded sadly, and shifted in her seat, preparing to stand.

"If we waited until the semester ended..." I heard myself say. I wasn't even completely sure I'd said the words aloud until I saw her expression change.

"I don't want to wait that long," she replied. "And if no one knows, it doesn't matter."

"We would know," I said.

She smiled shyly. "True. But there aren't rules about being friends, right?"

I gazed down at my desk as though the handbook for appropriate teacher-student relations were plastered to the wood. "No," I finally said. "So we could probably continue with that until the semester ends."

Her smile widened and the sparkle returned to her eyes. "Just no...touching," she said. "I can live with that."

I exhaled one more labored breath. I felt immensely happy and lighter already, but I was positively certain as I echoed her sentiment aloud that I had just taken the first step down a dangerous, dark path. I could not live with the rules we'd just established. And really, why would I want to?

She stood from her seat, smoothing her top over her flat abdomen. "I'll see you in class Thursday."

BRIDGET

Thursday couldn't come fast enough. On Wednesday evening, I scrutinized my closet for close to an hour, trying on countless outfits before selecting the one that best accentuated my assets without looking like I was trying too hard. It needed to signal that I was capable of being just friends while still reminding Owen that we both wanted much, much more.

I ended up with patterned tights, a corduroy skirt, and a fitted sweater. It was cute and sassy but not overtly sexy. I wore my hair down, and having slept with it in a damp braid the night before, the shiny locks formed smooth, loose waves. I arrived at class a few minutes early, just like I always did, and pulled out my notepad, day planner, and favorite pen, just like I always did.

When I dared to glance up, Owen was staring back at me, grinning widely. He turned away once our eyes met, but I already had butterflies. He was wearing gray slacks and a button down plaid shirt. The sleeves were rolled up, revealing his strong forearms. He started class at the chalkboard, giving me—and likely every other female in the class

—ample opportunity to check out his ass without raising suspicion. Then as he began to discuss the portion of the lesson on culture, he casually perched on the front edge of his desk.

There was nothing openly sexual or even unusual about his position, and I realized most other professors likely tired of standing at some point and similarly sat on their desk. But seeing him like that, his legs spread about hip width apart, drove me wild. I wished the rest of the class would disappear and I could stand flush against him, nestled right into that space between his thighs.

Class ended long before I wanted it to. My classmates had all started to pack up their books when Owen interrupted the quiet chatter that had begun throughout the room.

"The Italian club is showing a movie in the theater room on the ninth floor of this building Tuesday night at eight. I'd love to see you all there," he said.

"Will we get extra credit?" Jerrod asked from the back of the room.

Owen laughed. "It's a great movie. *La Grande Bellezza*. You should come because it'll be a blast and you'll learn more about Italian culture and language."

A mousy girl I'd never really noticed raised her hand, frowning. "So, no extra credit?"

"I could be persuaded to give extra credit to students who attend and then write a paragraph or two telling me what they learned about Italy from the movie," he said. This elicited some happy remarks from the students, who all filed out quickly. The mousy girl was slow to leave, so I dropped my notebook, letting all the papers flutter out. I figured by the time I picked everything up, I'd be alone with Owen.

Unfortunately, Jerrod saw my "accident" and rushed over to help.

"I got it, thanks," I said, but he continued to help. It

figured that he chose this moment to start being a gentleman.

His back was to Owen, and as I glanced up past Jerrod, I realized Owen was watching us, struggling to stifle a laugh.

"Will I see you there Tuesday, then, Jerrod?" Owen asked.

Jerrod shrugged. "Maybe. You going, Bridget?"

I shoved everything back into my backpack and glanced over at Owen. "I could be persuaded," I said.

CHAPTER 9

BRIDGET

*D*isappointed with the lack of contact or interaction with Owen on Thursday, I returned to my sorority and tried to unwind with a book of sonnets. I knew it was totally dorky, but I'd read it so many times that I could fully lose myself in the familiar words on the pages. I loved the rhythm of the poems, how they flowed quickly but with a fixed pace, like a song. And I loved that not a single syllable was wasted. Rather, every last word had been painstakingly hand-chosen to convey an exact sentiment that somehow still rang true two hundred years later.

As I finally shut the book, resigned to spend a little time on actual homework, an idea came to me.

OWEN

On Tuesday morning, I eagerly awaited the start of my class. I'd always enjoyed teaching, as impossible as that sounded, but since meeting Bridget, I'd anticipated certain classes with an excitement typically reserved for children on Christmas Eve. At each class, it was a treat to see how Bridget would look at me, what she was wearing, how her hair would be styled, whether she'd talk in class, and how much she would fidget. But that day, she brought me a literal present.

She waltzed into the class and headed directly for my desk. I didn't even have a chance to worry about what she'd say, as she quickly plunked a book on the desk. I glanced down to see it was a collection of Shakespearian sonnets.

"I found this book in the hall," she said, her almond-shaped eyes fixed on mine. "I thought maybe you could track down the owner."

Then she winked and quickly returned to her desk. I smiled and began class, unable to stop thinking about the book.

Once safely in the privacy of my office with the door shut, I flung open the book. I quickly confirmed my suspicion that it was hers, rather than a lost book, based on her swirly printing inside the front cover. I flipped through the book, flattered that she'd trust me with what I imagined to be a favorite of hers, when a small slip of paper slid out. It was a note. It was neither addressed to me nor signed by her, but I recognized the handwriting as hers.

As a friend, I thought you might enjoy this book. I've marked my favorites, but will forgive you if you prefer others. I'm still a sucker for his plays, but you can't deny the simple perfection of Shakespeare's sonnets. Maybe someday I'll relax with this book on a wrought iron balcony above a sparkling Venetian canal lined by ages- old cobblestone paths and I'll form a new perspective on these poems. But until then, I'll probably settle for reading on a cozy bench under a tree on the west side of campus. If you ever see a girl hiding on that bench with a box of Hot Tamales weeping over a play she's read a hundred times before, it's probably me. I'm heading to a movie the Italian club is showing tonight so if you want to talk, find me there.

I smiled. Her note was perfect. It was sweet and subtle, but revealed a lot about her. I quickly flipped to her favorites, a plan forming in my mind.

BRIDGET

That night, I convinced Stella to come to the movie with me. Jerrod had offered to meet up beforehand, but I really didn't want to risk committing to attend and having him think it was a date. Still, when we arrived, we sat by him, if only to be polite. Stella sure didn't mind and quickly started chatting with him, giving me the omg-he-is-hot look every time Jerrod glanced away. I was glad they'd hit it off and quickly excused myself to buy popcorn.

I immediately spotted the popcorn, but instead turned the other way, more interested in finding Owen. As I rounded a corner, I literally bumped into him. The full-on contact against his tall, hard body was unnerving but in a really, really good way.

"Ms. Williams," he said, smiling.

"Professor Chambers," I replied.

"You leaving already?"

"Just looking for popcorn."

He raised an eyebrow, and I had to admit the sound of the commercial air popper churning out the kernels was comically loud. He reached into his coat pocket and handed me a box of Hot Tamales.

"I hear they go well with popcorn. If you ever find where they're hiding that," he teased.

I smiled, relieved he'd read my note. "Have you seen this movie before?"

He nodded. "I think you'll love it."

I was about to say something else when I noticed his stare shift to just past my shoulder. I turned to see Stella approaching. She was smiling like a schoolgirl. I stopped her before she said anything too embarrassing.

"Stella, this is Professor Chambers. He teaches my Italian class."

Her expression was clear that she hadn't realized he was a professor. Since he was young and hot, that was completely understandable.

"Sorry to interrupt," she said, blushing. "Nice to meet you."

"No interruption at all," he said. "Enjoy the movie, ladies."

I watched him walk off, disappointed, then realized Stella was gawking at him too.

"Omigod why don't any of my professors look like that?" she asked.

I giggled. "I know, right. And here you questioned why I'm taking Italian."

We laughed together and walked back to the popcorn. Stella had indeed hit it off with Jerrod but wanted to know if I liked him, too, before she flirted too heavily. I gave her the green light to move ahead full steam, then settled in my chair with my candy. When the lights turned out, I fixed my stare directly on Owen, seated across the room. By the end of the movie, he was staring back.

* * *

DURING CLASS ON THURSDAY, I felt immensely mature, as I made it through the entire class without entertaining a single inappropriate fantasy about the professor. After class though, he called my name. Several students were still in the classroom, chatting excitedly about their weekend activities, so I wasn't surprised that he didn't say anything too personal.

"Ms. Williams, you left this book here last class. I thought you should have it back," he said, without letting his face reveal any expression.

"Thank you," I replied, taking the book. I waited a moment, in case he wanted to add anything else, but he didn't.

When I got to my next class, I flipped through the book. I had marked half a dozen of my favorite sonnets, and next to each one was a piece of paper with what I assumed to be the Italian translations of each sonnet. I couldn't pronounce some of the words and wouldn't know what half of it meant without the English version right beside it, but even so, the words were powerful. I couldn't imagine a more passionate language than Italian and I would kill to hear Owen read these words aloud in that sexy accent of his. Next to the last poem, there was an additional handwritten note.

Thank you for sharing this book with me. I enjoyed the poems you marked, though I think they're equally beautiful in translation. Italian, not Latin (and certainly not English), is the true language for lovers, and therefore best suited for such poems.

Venetian canals are gorgeous, though often a disappointment to unsuspecting Americans. On your first visit, arrive in the morning, when the city is still quiet and clean. As the fishermen set out on their morning tasks, the canals sparkle more than any other time of day. The water isn't clear, but I find its darkness adds to the mystery and romance of it all. Despite that, I'm partial to the architecture of Italy. No other country has maintained such impeccable examples of architecture from so many different artistic periods as Italy. From Ancient Rome to the cathedrals of the medieval era, palaces from the Renaissance, to modern museums, you'll find it all there. Along with plenty of benches for reading.

I RE-READ THE NOTE TWICE, then slammed the book shut as my next class began.

That night, I spent twice as long drafting my next letter to Owen as I did on all of my other assignments combined. Granted this letter was longer than my others, reaching a full three pages handwritten, but I'd written and rewritten some paragraphs more times than I ever would've revised a term paper. And unable to wait any longer to deliver it, I made a detour by his office hours the very next day. I made sure no one was in his office, then waltzed in, dropped it on his desk, and exited without a word.

The benefit of delivering the note then was that I received a response by the next class. Owen's letter was similarly lengthy, although his delved into some tedious and decidedly unromantic topics, like the looming deadline for the Florence study abroad program. I wished he'd stick to translations of romantic poetry into Italian, but I supposed there was some benefit to hearing reality, too.

The thing that really caught my attention was the postscript. First off, he actually wrote "postscript." I wasn't sure I'd actually realized before what the "p.s." even stood for in a letter, so there was an infinite charm to him writing it out. He mentioned that he had some research to do for some article he was attempting to write. He noted the precise floor and wing of the library where he'd be researching the following evening, and the general time.

He ended his letter saying, "If you do come to the library then, bring lots of paper. Passing notes is a necessity in the library as talking is forbidden."

I giggled at his terminology, certain that speaking near the study carols wasn't the real forbidden fruit tempting us both. But I played along, packing a crisp new notepad and a purple glitter gel pen.

I arrived at the designated time and place and, true to his word, Owen was there, diligently reading some enormous book. When I appeared, he smiled and nodded his head in the direction of an empty desk. I sat, noting that there were books and a pen on the desk beside me. Owen gestured to the stacks across the aisle, where an older man was standing and reading a dusty anthology.

Hence the notes, I decided.

I pulled out my own homework, opting for multitasking, and pointedly started with Italian. I zipped through my conjugations, acutely aware that Owen was reading my paper based on the changes in his breathing when I got one wrong. By the time I finished my Italian, a note landed on my book.

I read it and giggled, then wrote back, dropping it onto Owen's desk just as the other man returned. He nodded politely at me, then Owen, and then packed up his items. A moment later, Owen's reply came sailing across the desk to me.

I sighed, then scribbled another note. "This is ridiculously inefficient. Let's continue this conversation at your apartment. I promise I'll behave."

I watched his expression as he read the note, but he gave away no clues. I held my breath as I opened the paper with his response, praying he agreed, but instead all he'd written was "I won't."

I bit my lip, too amused and flattered to be disappointed, but when I gazed up, the look in his eyes was scorching. I felt my face heat up, followed quickly by the rest of my body. I was torn. His words said no, but his body very much so seemed to be saying yes. It was maddening.

"Good. I don't want you to behave," I wrote back.

I dropped the note on his desk as I walked off towards the stacks, wondering if I could find some love poems or something else to read in front of him to taunt him. I sucked at finding books in the library without a specific call number, though, so I was very slowly gazing at the selection on a specific shelf when a figure blocked the light from the window at the end of the aisle.

Owen rushed to me before I could think straight. He placed his finger over his lip shushing me, then gestured towards a partially hidden camera with his head. He walked to the opposite end of the aisle then stopped, reached for me, and kissed me hard on the lips.

"If we are alone together, I won't be able to not touch you," he said.

I simply stared at him, my body still tingling from the kiss.

He appeared to be having some sort of internal dialogue that resulted in a myriad of facial expressions. Finally, he shook his head. "It's number 1284. I'll leave the door unlocked. But I think it's better if you just go home."

He left as quickly as he'd appeared, leaving me shaking my head. Did he really think I could've forgotten his address?

OWEN

I packed up my books and left the library in a hurry, grateful I was able to park in the close lot. I was certain I'd just made a huge mistake, but I didn't really care. Bridget wasn't just some tease, flirting with her professor because she could. Her interest was sincere, as was mine. I couldn't shake the feeling that I was about to become a cliché, so I kept reminding myself that I'd already slept with her once. At this point, it wasn't like I was doing anything worse.

As soon as I got home, I started tidying up. I wasn't a slob, but I didn't have a cleaning service either, and my apartment showed it. I'd already taken care with my own appearance, knowing I would see her, but it legitimately hadn't occurred to me she might come back to my apartment. Clearly I'd overestimated my own willpower.

By the time I'd been home for a full half hour, I started to wonder if maybe she actually wasn't coming. Right then, there was a soft knock on the door, and the door swung open. Bridget stepped in quickly and shut the door behind her, suddenly looking shy.

"I thought maybe you'd come to your senses and weren't going to show up," I said.

"Well, here I am," she replied, shrugging and cocking her head to the side.

Suddenly, I was nervous, too. "You want a drink? I have soda, water, beer…" my voice trailed off as I realized I didn't even know if she was twenty-one. Now in addition to being the professor seducing his students, I could be that professor sneaking beer to the minors, too. She looked twenty-one, but she was only a junior, so…

"No thanks," she said.

I retreated to the kitchen to get myself a glass of water regardless. For some reason, my mouth was now dry. When I returned, Bridget was staring at the different pictures throughout the living room.

"Is this your grandma's house in Italy?"

I nodded. "Yes. I mean, it's the one she grew up in. It's not in the family anymore."

"Tell me more about that summer you spent there as a kid," she said, relaxing onto the couch. She slipped her shoes off and pulled her feet up beside her, her elbow propped on the arm of the couch with her head resting against the palm of her hand.

She looked so effortlessly beautiful that it was almost hard to focus. But she'd asked me to tell her about my summer in Italy, so I did. I sat in the armchair adjacent to the couch and rambled on. When I ran out of things to tell her about that trip, she asked about my undergraduate years, my study abroad in Italy, and my work so far. Then she asked what sparked my love of architecture.

When I glanced at the clock, I realized I'd been talking for over an hour and had learned nothing new about her.

"I'm sorry," I said. "I did not intend to ramble on so much. You must be bored."

She shook her head, smiling sweetly. "Not in the least. You are fascinating. And you have a soothing voice."

I laughed, wondering if she was implying I nearly put her to sleep. "I wouldn't mind hearing more about you," I said. "Unless you need to get back."

Bridget didn't tear her eyes away. "I have no place to be until class tomorrow. Italian 300 taught by a hunky guy with dimples to die for."

I couldn't help but flash the dimples she referenced. "So really, tell me something I don't know about you."

She shifted on the couch, twisted her hair into a knot behind her head, then sighed. "That's hard. I'm not that interesting."

"I'm interested," I said.

She laughed. "Okay, well I have two younger brothers, I love music, baseball, and hopelessly romantic poems and tragic love stories."

"Tell me something I don't know."

"Okay, here's a bit of trivia. I have never held a job."

I considered her statement. "Never?"

She shook her head.

"What about babysitting or something like that? An after school job in high school?"

"Nothing," she said. "Well, I guess I babysat my little brothers, but I don't think that really counts."

"So, are you here on academic scholarship?" I asked, now curious as to how she was paying tuition.

She laughed louder now, clearly thinking this was a preposterous conclusion. "No. Despite never working, I also don't have good enough grades for a scholarship." She paused. "But my parents are wealthy. My father is a lawyer, and I am a total daddy's girl."

I felt a little nervous at the mention of her father's career, but she didn't pause long enough for me to question it.

"My parents pay my tuition, my housing, and my other expenses. They bought my car, pay my insurance and my cell phone bill. They even fund my manicures." She wiggled her hot pink fingernails. "Do you hate me now?"

"Why would I hate you?"

"Because I'm completely unrelatable. Everything has been handed to me on a silver spoon and therefore I lack character."

I couldn't believe she actually felt this way about herself. "It's not something to be ashamed of, your family having money."

She shrugged.

"But let's go back to this part about your dad being a lawyer. It seems like Daddy may not like his little girl hanging out with a creepy older associate professor."

Bridget smiled. "That's part of the beauty of college. Daddy doesn't always know exactly what I'm up to. And I don't necessarily always do what he would like."

I sat back, licking my lips as I watched her fidget with her bracelet.

She caught me staring and abruptly stilled her fingers. "Keeping my hands busy distracts me," she explained.

"From?" I prompted.

She rolled her eyes. "I promised to behave."

The muscles all along my midsection tightened. I thought about reminding her of everything we had to lose and that the semester wasn't so long that we couldn't wait, but, instead, I didn't say anything. I just kept thinking about that kiss in my car, how frantically her hands had moved along my arm, how perfect her body felt in my hands.

"But I didn't," I said.

I stood slowly from my seat, watching Bridget and carefully gauging her expression. I held my hand out to her and she quickly accepted it, letting me tug her gently to her feet. She was shorter than me, but not impossibly so. When I looked down and she tilted her head up, we were the perfect heights for...well, for everything we shouldn't be doing. I waited a moment, enjoying the feel of her soft hand in mine and the pleading expression in her vivid eyes.

I leaned in slowly, savoring every second while also allowing ample time for her to slap me and walk away. When our lips finally did make contact, Bridget sighed contentedly, reminding me of a kitten purring. We kissed tenderly, a stark contrast from the frantic kissing in the car. This time, it was like we were each desperate to memorize every inch of each other's lips.

As the kiss deepened, I dropped her hand, raising my hands to her cheeks instead. She followed suit but reached around my back, her hands nudging me closer until her body was pressed against mine. God she felt good. Every part of her was a dream come true. I reached my hands around her back, needing to feel more of her body under my skin, then realized I missed the feeling of her hair wrapping around my fingers.

Not breaking contact with our mouths, I tugged on the elastic holding her hair in place, smiling against her lips as her hair tumbled freely around us. Her hair was so silky and soft, and I loved the feeling of it tangled between my fingers as I pulled her closer and closer. Her hands settled along my ass, so I moved mine to hers. But one touch of her perky, firm ass, even through the thick denim jeans she wore, was enough to drive me wild. My dick was hard as a rock, and since she was pressed tightly against me, I was sure she knew it. She ground her hips against me, mewing softly again in response to the increased friction, and giving me all the encouragement I needed to take things one step further.

I slid my hands up to the hem of her shirt and tugged it over her head, pulling back to let the shirt pass, then to check out her glorious chest. I returned my lips to her body, but this time starting at her neck, kissing and sucking my way down her body. I kissed the tops of her breasts that jutted out above her bra and gazed up at her for permission to continue. Her eyes were closed, but she thrust her hands into my hair, holding me close.

I unfastened her bra and slipped it off her arms before kissing her on the mouth again, keeping enough distance between our bodies to place my hands over her supple breasts. I squeezed gently, then traced a finger around her nipples, which instantly hardened at my touch. Her breathing increased rapidly, and I again worked my lips down her body. I kissed and licked her breasts for a moment, her reaction so noticeable that I almost wondered if she'd come from that alone.

Then I reached for her jeans, unfastening them without moving my mouth from her breast. I shimmied her jeans over her hips and left my hands on her breasts while moving my lips across her abdomen to her stomach. I dropped to my knees and licked her firmly through her lace panties. Her hips bucked against me and her eyes shot open. I grinned, slipped her panties down to her thighs and dug my fingers into her hips, holding her against me as I feasted on her damp epicenter.

Her breath quickened and her fingers tightened around my hair. I focused my tongue right along her clit for another moment, reaching my finger up to pinch her nipple at the same time and she came, loudly and violently. I knew the gentlemanly thing to do would be to slow down, to let her take a minute and recover, maybe think about whether she wanted to do any more, but I couldn't wait. I had never been so aroused in my entire life. Well, or at least since the last time we were intimate.

I lowered her onto the couch, tugged her panties off over her feet, then yanked my shirt over my head. I unfastened my pants while racing to the bedroom for a condom, half afraid I'd return and realize this was all just a dream. But instead, when I returned, she was still draped across my couch, a wanton smile on her face and not a single thread of clothing. I stripped out of my pants and boxer briefs and tossed her the condom, deciding that would be her opportunity to turn me down.

Instead, she ripped the foil packet open and bent one knee, propping it up along the couch. I lunged for her, letting her slowly sheath me while I desperately tried to control my breathing in hopes of holding out long enough to let her find her pleasure again first.

I positioned myself at her entrance, hovering over her. "You sure?" I panted.

She raised her hips in response, bridging the small gap between us. I needed no further affirmation, filling her fully on the first thrust. She moaned loudly, eagerly meeting me thrust for thrust. I had meant to be gentle and slow, but instead I slammed into her over and over again, harder and harder until the pressure building inside of me was nearly unbearable. At that moment I felt her nails dig into my back and her pussy tightened rhythmically around my dick, pushing me over the edge. I came hard, filling the condom with such force that I prayed it didn't burst.

I collapsed on top of her, needing a moment to recover before I could even pull out.

"Jesus," I mumbled.

She sighed happily. "You are really good at that."

I laughed, too spent to even return the compliment. Clearly, she had to know I felt the same. I hadn't even realized sex could be that good.

"I should go," she said after a few more minutes.

I frowned. I was, quite literally, still inside her, and here she was trying to bail. This couldn't be a good sign. I picked up my head to face her, hoping to get a read on her mood.

She smiled. "Unless you want me to spend the night and just ride with you to class tomorrow in the same clothes I wore today," she said.

"Shit."

I slowly shifted off of her and disposed of the condom by wrapping it in a tissue and tossing it into the trash can.

"You don't have to leave now," I said.

"It's after eleven o'clock."

I jerked up faster. "Seriously?

She laughed. "Yes."

I scrambled around, tossing her random articles of clothing. She stood, stretched while still completely naked, then stepped into her panties and began dressing.

"It's almost like you know how good you look," I said.

"Owen, the way you look at me, I feel like the sexiest woman alive."

I smiled. "You should. And you are."

I pulled on my boxer briefs and my jeans but didn't mess with my shirt.

"I'm glad you didn't behave," she said, leaning over to kiss me. "I'll see you tomorrow morning."

All I could do was nod.

CHAPTER 10

BRIDGET

I was less distracted than usual in class the next day. Maybe because I was finally satiated, for the moment anyway. As I walked into the class, Owen handed me a note. I didn't notice anyone watching me, but just to be on the safe side, I waited a moment to unfold it.

It was a phone number, labeled "personal, private cell."

I smiled, waiting until after class to text him. "Thank you for the number. Didn't you like my handwritten notes though?"

"Very much so," he replied. "Please continue those. But this seems more convenient, and should be safe as long as no names are used."

"Or pics, I guess, right? If I send you sexy pics, it'll defeat purpose of avoiding names," I typed back.

I waited a minute, but there was no response.

"You still there?" I wrote.

"Yes. Still weighing risks. No. Decided risk of sexy pics outweighs benefits of anonymity."

I laughed. I was tempted to ask what he was doing that night, but didn't. I clearly wasn't playing hard to get, but I didn't need to smother him either. Besides, even though Stella somehow bought my explanation that I was at the library so late the prior night, there was no way she'd believe it again.

"Will have to wait. Busy now," I typed.

He replied with a pouty face, but then there was nothing from him the rest of that day, or the next day.

On Sunday, I texted him a picture of an iconic balcony in Florence. He replied with a quote from an Italian poet Giacomo Taldegardo. I hadn't heard of the guy, but looking into translations of some of his poems and essays from the 1800s occupied me for a good portion of the afternoon.

On Tuesday, the department head came to observe Owen teaching, so I sat in the back and behaved. By the time I returned to my sorority that evening after all of my classes though, I was itching to see him again. So, an hour before class on Thursday, I sent him another text in hopes of making him as desperate to be alone with me as I felt about him.

"Wanna play a game? It's called Guess What I'm Not Wearing to Class Today."

His reply was delayed. I suspected he was in a meeting, or grading, or doing whatever else teachers do shortly before class.

I was already on campus and walking into the building when I received the response.

"I guess ridiculously high-heeled shoes" was the text.

I gasped. "None of my shoes are ridiculous."

"First time I saw you. Ridiculous."

"Jerk. Well, now you may never know."

"Won't I be able to tell?"

"The particular item I'm not wearing isn't visible when I'm dressed."

He didn't reply. I continued my walk but when I reached the classroom, Owen was seated at his desk, his face flushed. When he saw me, he laughed aloud and shook his head.

I smiled proudly as I sauntered to a desk.

My phone buzzed after a moment. "You don't play fair," his text read.

I grinned wider and silenced my phone, wedging it back into my purse.

I was a tad distracted during class by my own attempts to repeatedly gauge how distracted Owen was.

At the end of class, I was eager to go subtly flirt with Owen but before I even stood up, Jack Pierson was looming over my desk.

I glanced up slowly, confused as to what he needed. He was a total jock. We'd lived in the same dorm freshman year, and run into each other a few times at parties since then, but we didn't exactly hang out with the same crowd. He was on the university's baseball team, so when we'd chatted in the past, it always tended to focus on our mutual love for the Cubs. And aside from our group outing to the Italian festival, I didn't think he'd said more than a few words to me since the start of the semester.

He sat on the desk beside me and smiled.

I returned the smile, still perplexed.

"So um, do you have anything planned this weekend?"

My eyes widened, as I tried to recall if there was something specific I should know about.

"Nothing special, really," I replied slowly.

He shrugged, as though trying to act casual, but his posture and voice seemed far from casual. "There are a couple of parties this weekend. Maybe I'll see you at one?"

I nodded. "Yeah, definitely." I glanced down, wincing. Why had I added 'definitely'? I didn't even know what parties he was talking about. It was a college campus, for Christ's sake. There were dozens of parties every weekend night.

"Cool. We could go together if that works for you?"

I froze. How had I not realized he was attempting to ask me out? I glanced over his shoulder, to where Owen was packing his own items into a brown leather messenger bag, clearly moving as slowly as he possibly could. This was awkward. In another time, I probably would've said yes. Jack was cute, athletic, and he liked the Cubs. He likely was not my soul mate, but there was nothing offensive about him, so even a semester ago, I easily could've seen myself giving him a chance. But now, no way.

I couldn't flat out reject him, so I tried to tactfully answer so as not to lead him on. "I need to double check whether my roommate was banking on a ride from me anywhere this weekend," I said lamely. "Umm if you text me the details on your party, I'll try to make it if I can, though."

Jack looked slightly dejected, but perked right up when I smiled. I started out of the classroom, having given up hope on talking with Owen now. Jack followed me out of the classroom like a lost puppy.

"Do you have another class now?"

"Not until after lunch."

"You want to go grab a bite?"

I glanced back at Owen, hoping he was out of ear shot now. "Um, sure."

I told myself that lunch with a friend who happened to be a guy would, if anything, comfort Owen. I didn't want him to think I was totally obsessed and I didn't want to be so obvious that other people started suspecting something. Besides, it was lunch, not a date. We went to the food court in the student union and each got our own food separately, then sat at a table in the center of the room. We made harmless, friendly conversation until I finished my salad, and then I excused myself to go study.

I ducked into the reading room and pulled out a book, but then checked my phone. Nothing from Owen. I decided to text him.

"You never guessed correctly," I wrote.

"You back from your date?" he replied. "Did Jack guess right?"

Ouch. "Smartass," I wrote. "Oh wait, you said no names..."

"Fine. I have a guess but need visual confirmation of answer. When are you free?"

"6?"

"Works for me."

* * *

AT SIX ON THE DOT, I burst into Owen's apartment. I dropped my backpack and leaned closer for a kiss, not wanting to waste any time.

Owen stepped back and shook his head. "Not until you read this," he said, thrusting a paper at me.

I pouted but accepted the paper and gave it a curious once-over. It was a printout from the university's student handbook. I rolled my eyes and held the paper out for Owen. "Not necessary," I said.

He snatched the paper back and began to read aloud. "Sexual relationships between students and faculty are strictly prohibited. A student engaged in a sexual relationship with any faculty member, whether or not the faculty member has any supervisory or educational authority over that particular student, may be subject to immediate expulsion."

Owen glanced up at me again. "Immediate expulsion," he repeated.

I shrugged. That was basically what I had assumed, although it seemed to suggest it didn't matter if I was a current student of said faculty member, and that part surprised me.

"The campus has a zero tolerance policy for sexual harassment," Owen continued, skipping over the lengthy and over-inclusive definition of sexual harassment. "If a student feels that he or she has been the victim of sexual harassment by any member of the faculty, he or she should immediately report the incident to the Department of Student Services. All such complaints will be investigated, maintaining the anonymity of the complaining student to the extent possible."

Owen stopped reading and glanced at me to see if I was listening. "I'd really feel better if you'd just read the whole thing."

His expression told me he was serious, so I accepted the paper, sat at the table, and read it. When I was done, I glanced up. He was watching me expectantly. Honestly, I was a little insulted that he seemed to think I hadn't known all that already, but it was sweet that he was so concerned.

"This changes nothing," I said, adding, "And I'm not turning you in for sexual harassment either."

He sat beside me. "Bridget, you've got to understand, my job is to help you further your academic career. What we're doing—what I'm doing—could end your academic career. I need to know that you understand that, and that you know I'm serious when I say that we can end this now and it will have no effect on your grade or other classes in the department or anything."

"Whatever the penalties are for me, I'm sure the risks for you are a lot greater. If you get caught, they'd fire you, and then all that time in graduate school would be for nothing."

Owen smiled. "It's worth it."

I frowned. "Grad school was that fun?"

He laughed. "Not grad school, you."

I climbed out of my chair and onto his lap. "Professor Chambers, I think that comment of yours constitutes an inappropriate innuendo in violation of section 4.3-5(b) of the University Code of Conduct."

He grinned, but still looked worried. "So, Jack..."

I shrugged. "A friend. More like an acquaintance, really."

"He asked you out."

I laughed. "Yeah. That was awkward."

Owen frowned.

"I'm not going out with him," I replied.

He shifted beneath me. "If you want to, you should. He seems like a decent kid, he's not your professor, and doesn't he have a shot at the major leagues or something? Your mother would love him."

"I'm not sure he's that good. But no, I don't want to go out with Jack. I'm interested in someone else. And normally, when a guy asks me out, I'd just tell him that I liked someone else, if that were, in fact, the reason I was saying no. But I didn't feel that was appropriate because then he'd want to know who the other guy was."

"This is exactly why policies like this exist," Owen said, shaking the printout from the university website in his hand. "So that pervy professors don't get crushes on hot female students and then flunk nice guys who hit on the hot female student."

"You're going to flunk Jack?"

Owen rolled his eyes. "No, of course not. Aside from you he's actually one of my best students. But the point is that I shouldn't feel jealous of a student."

I smiled. As stupid as it was, jealousy turned me on a little. I mean, the innocent kind of jealousy. If taken too far, I could definitely see it being annoying rather than endearing.

Owen still looked stressed, which was frustrating. I had hoped my panty-free day would lead to a fun, lighthearted evening, not some deep talk.

I leaned back and started to unbutton my shirt. By the time I got halfway through with the buttons, Owen was looking much less concerned about the ethics of our relationship.

"So you're definitely wearing a bra," he commented, reaching under my blouse to caress me through the silky fabric of my bra.

My breath hitched and I struggled to finish with the buttons while he was still fondling my breasts. He breathed a laugh.

"I'll help," he offered, quickly removing my shirt for me.

I helped him out of his shirt then stood. "What was your guess again?" I teased, my fingers poised at the waistband of my pants. They were thick, fitted black pants—a slight step above leggings, but still no buttons or zipper to mess with.

Owen swallowed visibly then reached out and groped my butt, running his fingers between my legs and grinning. "What's my prize if I'm right?" he asked, tugging me closer and kissing my belly.

I giggled, letting him slide my pants off. Then I pulled him to his feet, and stripped him before nudging him back into the chair. Making love in the chair brought some added benefits- easy access for Owen's mouth to my breasts, which was phenomenal, and more control for me, which was fun. But I decided I sort of preferred when he took the lead and devoured me like a cake he couldn't wait to enjoy.

I tried to stand from the chair right after, but Owen pulled me back onto his lap.

"What's in the backpack? Did you come straight from class?"

I shook my head. "I thought it would help convince Stella I was studying."

"On a Thursday night?" he said skeptically. "Thought when you don't have Friday classes the weekend starts early."

"Okay, well I also packed some clothes for tomorrow on the off chance I happened to sleep over," I said, not wanting to presume I was even invited.

Thankfully, Owen smiled. "Good. I'm thinking we should order pizza, then maybe get you into the shower, then probably go to bed really early." He paused. "Wait, won't she notice if you're out all night?"

I shrugged. "She has a date. She might be out all night too."

Owen cringed. "Jerrod?"

I nodded. We discussed pizza options and then I started to shower.

A few minutes into my shower, there was a knock at the door, and then Owen appeared.

"I thought you might need help finding the shampoo," he explained.

I giggled nervously. I had already checked out his hair products and for a guy, it wasn't bad. I hadn't expected him to be a shampoo/body wash/conditioner all-in-one sort of guy, but a girl could never be positive.

"Mind if I join you?"

"It's your shower," I said.

He stepped into the shower, quickly overwhelming me. It was a shower-tub combo, but even so, the space felt small for the both of us. He grabbed the body wash I was holding and lathered some up on his hands before rubbing it into my shoulders, down my arms, then back up my abdomen and over my breasts.

My breath hitched. Owen laughed mischievously and continued to slip his hands back and forth over my body, focusing on the most sensitive parts. He moved behind me, reaching around to continue his playful torture of my nipples. Suddenly his right hand moved lower. He nudged my feet further apart with his own foot and then slid his palm over the apex where my legs met. My head flopped to the side and he seized the opportunity to kiss and suck the side of my neck, distracting me as his finger slipped into my body.

I moaned as he slowly withdrew his finger, traced it along my opening, then thrust it back into me. I braced myself against the shower wall, feeling dizzy and weak with pleasure already. When I finally exploded with overwhelming waves of pleasure, Owen held tight to me with his left hand, clearly afraid I'd collapse

We had just shut off the water when there was a knock at the door followed by a sharp ringing. I quickly snapped out of my post-orgasm bliss and started to panic.

"Pizza," Owen said with a laugh, quickly draping a towel around himself. "Stay here."

He scurried out of the bathroom, presumably hunting for his pants. "Coming!" he hollered.

I stepped out of the shower and wrapped his bath robe around me, finding no other towel. I used the hand towel to dry my hair, then combed my fingers through the long tresses before hunting through my backpack for a few of my essential products. I was grateful for the moment alone, not because I thought Owen would judge me for the pricey hair serum I couldn't live without, or my moisturizer, or the way I awkwardly braided my own hair when I wouldn't have time to blow dry it. Rather, I needed a minute of privacy because I was overwhelmed.

I really, really liked Owen. Being with him felt good and

oh so right. But he was my professor. This couldn't last forever, and when it ended, it would be awkward. Worse than awkward, actually. Tragic. I was torn between seeking to protect my heart and throwing myself fully into the affair so I could enjoy it while it lasted. Plus, spending the night was a big step. I'd never slept over with a man except Patrick, my ex. And even then, we'd only had a couple full nights alone together since he was in a frat and I was in a sorority.

There was a soft tap at the door and then Owen poked his head in. "You okay?"

I nodded.

"Oh, sorry. I have other towels in the cabinet there," he said, gesturing. "I'm not used to company."

I smiled. That was a good thing. "Should I not wear this?" I asked, gesturing to the robe.

He stepped closer and kissed the tip of my nose. "You may wear, or not wear, whatever you want." As he spoke, he tugged on the belt, causing the robe to fall open. His eyes widened and he grinned widely.

"You are so gorgeous. You know that, right?"

I felt myself blush right as my stomach growled loudly.

Owen laughed. "Come on, let's get you fed."

I slipped into the panties I'd kept in my backpack and then glanced around his bedroom, quickly finding a stack of undershirts. I grabbed a sleeveless black one and slipped it over my head then wrapped the robe back around me.

When I met him in the kitchen, he had set out real plates and paper napkins. "Help yourself," he said, so I did.

"Drink?" he asked. "I've got beer, soda, bourbon…" His voice trailed off.

"Beer is fine," I said, noting that he'd already opened one for himself.

He opened a bottle for me and handed it to me, then

leaned back against the counter, an odd expression on his face. "How old are you?" he asked.

I laughed, realizing the man who'd brought me to orgasm at least once in nearly every room of his apartment was now concerned that he'd provided alcohol to a minor. "I turned twenty-one in October," I said.

"Oh thank God," he replied, his relief palpable.

I took a bite of pizza. "Really, you're that concerned you'd get caught for allowing underage drinking? That I'd keep the ridiculously good sex a secret but tell people you gave me beer?"

"Ridiculously good, huh?" he repeated.

I rolled my eyes and pretended to be fascinated by my pizza. "How old are you?"

"Guess."

I shook my head, but he didn't seem willing to tell, so I did the mental math in my head, and then subtracted a year from where I thought he must be so as not to offend him. "Thirty?"

He raised an eyebrow, and stuffed the rest of his slice into his mouth, leaving me in suspense while he chewed. "Not bad. But twenty-eight. Well, almost twenty-nine."

"Almost?"

"March 26," he said.

I made a mental note of this, not sure of how I would acknowledge his birthday but certain it would need some sort of recognition. "That's not that big of an age difference," I said finally.

Owen raised an eyebrow. "I could drive when you were still in elementary school."

Hmm. It did sound more significant when he phrased it that way.

I sipped my beer and focused on the pizza. Something told me I might need to keep my energy up for the rest of the night with my Italian stallion. From the other room, my phone chimed. I shoved another bite in my mouth then went to check my text.

It was Stella. She was having a fabulous time with Jerrod and wanted me not to wait up to hear about it. I smiled. For all the trouble she was, I wanted her to be happy.

"One of your boyfriends?" Owen asked, grinning mischievously behind me.

"Stella. We always check in at nine PM when one of us is on a date." I set my phone on the counter. "She won't be back tonight."

Owen stepped closer. "And no one else will notice you're gone?"

I shrugged. Someone might notice, but they certainly wouldn't think anything strange by it.

"And Stella doesn't know…"

It took me a moment to realize what he was asking, but once I figured it out, I shook my head vigorously.

"But she's your best friend."

I nodded. "We're not twelve though. I don't have to tell her everything. If it gets to the point where she starts to suspect something, I'll tell her I'm seeing someone but don't want to jinx it by saying who." I paused, taking in his worried face. "Owen, I understand the importance of keeping this just between us. You can trust me."

"I know, I know," he murmured, kissing the top of my head. "This is just all so out of character for me. I'm usually the responsible, boring one, making good decisions even when I really want something else."

I reached for my beer. "I'm not. I'm normally the fun one. I rarely make good decisions." I started towards the pizza box for another slice. "But I can keep a secret."

Owen chuckled. "Speaking of decisions, did you finish the application for the study abroad in Italy? We've only received two for that particular program, so I can almost guarantee you'd get accepted."

I sighed. The application was completed, signed, and carefully placed inside a folder in the backpack across the room. And the thought of spending a summer in Italy was lovely. If I could've turned in the paperwork in December, I would've done so in a heartbeat. But now...

"I thought I would apply but now I'm having second thoughts."

"What's changed?"

"My parents think I should study in France."

"You could do that, too. You could do a whole semester there next year if you wanted."

"If I went this summer, I'd be finished with my minor and wouldn't have to take any other classes on campus."

"I'd miss having you as a student, but that would simplify things," he said. Then he made a face and glanced down. "Not to assume we'd still be... well, it would just be easier either way."

I knew what he meant. Being my teacher during the day and sleeping with me at night was clearly a struggle. But no matter how things ended with us, it would be awkward to have class together as ex-lovers. Maybe in a huge lecture hall it would be different, but the higher level foreign language classes were small, some with less than fifteen students. But that exact awkwardness applied equally well in Italy.

"Summer is a long way off," I said, "and with everything that's happened with us, I just don't see how being in Italy together wouldn't be an issue."

Owen squeezed my arm. "Florence is a big city. I can stay out of your way as much or as little as you need me to when the time comes. Take me out of the equation entirely when you're deciding if you want to go. If you're not going because of me or despite me, it won't matter what's going on between us when the time comes."

I thought about his words for a minute and realized it made sense. I was dying to see Italy, really. More than I wanted to see France. And if Owen and I were no longer involved romantically then, well, I was confident there were plenty of hot Italian men I could get to know. I retrieved the application from my backpack and dropped it on his desk.

He grinned.

CHAPTER 11

OWEN

*M*y good mood hadn't faded by Tuesday, and I realized I was actually whistling to myself as I walked across campus. I hadn't seen Bridget since she left my bed Friday morning, but we'd exchanged a couple of texts over the weekend. She'd never actually called, though, so I was surprised when my phone started ringing and "private number" flashed across the screen.

"Good morning," she greeted perkily.

"Good morning to you," I replied, glancing around me to ensure no one could possibly hear my conversation. "You sound chipper."

"I am. I had a fantastic start to the weekend, and it is gorgeous outside today."

I gazed up. She was right about that. It was unseasonably warm, the sun was shining, and the sky was bright blue. "Aren't I going to see you soon?"

Her response was delayed. "Well, actually that's why I'm

calling. I'm not going to be in class today and I just didn't want you to worry or think it had anything to do with Thursday night."

I appreciated that heads up, as I probably would've panicked that her absence was a result of something I'd said or done or hadn't done during our last night together. "Okay, thanks for letting me know. Are you sick, or…" My voice trailed off. I couldn't think of another reason to miss class, but she sure didn't sound sick.

"Are you asking as my professor or as my friend?"

I frowned. "Does it make a difference?"

Bridget laughed. "Well if any of my other professors ask why I'm not in class today or tomorrow, I would tell them about this horrific, highly contagious stomach virus going around." She paused. "But if a friend were to ask, I'd probably say it's too gorgeous of a day to be cooped up in a classroom and that Stella and I are road tripping to Chicago to go see Coldplay."

"In concert?" I asked, stupidly thinking for a moment she was maybe meeting up with the band or something.

"Yes. Last minute ticket acquisition. We'll get a hotel someplace downtown after the show tonight."

This still perplexed me. I couldn't imagine just waking up and deciding, apparently based on nice weather, to ditch two days of classes and drive four plus hours to see a concert. Then again, I could see Bridget making that choice.

"There's nothing in your other classes you can't miss?"

Bridget laughed again. It was a melodic care-free laugh that conjured up visions of nuns scampering through a grassy hillside. "I might miss something, but I can't imagine I'll regret it. And wouldn't it be a real shame to miss something like a road trip to an awesome concert with my best friend just because of a silly old class?"

I sighed. "Have fun. I guess I'll see you Thursday?"

"I wouldn't miss it for the world," she said, hanging up.

BRIDGET

I sensed Owen didn't completely agree with my decision to ditch classes to head to Chicago, but I reasoned it put him in an awkward position. I hadn't wanted the guy I was more than friends with to worry about my absence, but I didn't expect my professor to endorse skipping classes. I texted him a picture of the sky in Chicago when we arrived, showing him it was just as gorgeous there as on campus that day, but otherwise we didn't talk while I was gone.

The concert was fabulous, obviously. Stella and I may have done a tad too much pre-partying and a bit more partying after the concert, so we were both nursing epic hangovers as we roamed Michigan Avenue around lunchtime Wednesday. We shopped for a few hours, then headed back to campus.

The next day, Jerrod mobbed me as soon as I entered the classroom, having known from Stella where we'd been, so I perched on the edge of my desk and scrolled through my pictures from the concert with him and Jack until the hunky Professor Chambers called class to begin.

After class, Jerrod wanted to resume our chat, but I told him I needed to hit up the professor's office hours since I'd missed class. I headed straight up to Owen's office, but he was already talking with another student, the doors and blinds to his office firmly shut. So I sat down in the hall and tried to do some catch up homework.

The student before me left Owen's office looking as cheerful as I felt, so I assumed they were able to work out a deal on whatever exam or essay grade the student was contesting. I rapped on the side of the door and Owen indicated I should come in without glancing up to see who he was inviting.

I shut the door behind me and cleared my throat. He looked up and immediately broke into a wide smile.

"Excuse me, professor, but I have an issue with that last grade you gave me," I said coyly, perching on the edge of his cluttered desk.

He cocked an eyebrow. "You don't like A's?"

"I like to work hard to earn them," I replied.

Owen flushed. "My office hours end in ten minutes. I don't know how hard I can work you in that amount of time."

"Are you willing to stay late?"

"I think I could arrange that," he replied, leaning closer. He kissed me, thrusting his hands into my hair and nudging my mouth open with his tongue. I groaned softly and he pulled back as suddenly as he'd started the kiss.

"This is the longest semester ever," he mumbled.

I smiled, still quivering and catching my breath from the kiss. I sat in the chair across from his desk and he returned to his own seat. "The reason I came by, actually, was to share some good news."

Owen raised an eyebrow.

"I was accepted into the summer study program in Florence."

He pounded the desk with his fist. "Already? That's fantastic!"

I shrugged, equally thrilled.

"And your parents are okay with it all?"

"Yeah. My mom thought it was strange that I wasn't going to France, but I told her I could save that for graduate school. They're even going to pay for the program and my flight."

"Bridget that's great. I'm really happy for you," he said

sincerely. "I really think you're going to love Italy and the classes."

"I hear the new professor isn't too shabby either."

"It's too soon to tell, really, but said professor does have some experience traveling around Italy, if anyone is interested in extending their trip by a week or two."

I hesitated, uncertain if he was proposing we travel together or simply informing me of his plans to lead a group tour. "My parents thought I should visit France briefly, too, and maybe just tour Italy on the weekends when I don't have class."

"I would love to explore France," Owen replied, his eyes dark and suggestive.

"Are you saying you would escort me on my travels around France?"

He nodded, adding "And Italy."

I tilted my head. "You will technically be my professor in Italy, correct?"

Owen shrugged. "One of them. But European countries have very different views on this sort of relationship."

"My parents were anxious about the prospect of me visiting foreign cities alone."

"You would definitely be safer with a man by your side."

I couldn't stop smiling at him. He was so cute when he flirted, and, frankly, the possibility of being with him in Europe nearly compensated for the pain of being publicly apart from him all semester.

He narrowed his eyes further, shooting me a mischievous grin.

"What?"

"I think Paris might be the perfect city to start in. Could you fly there a week or two before your program and meet up with me there?"

"Why Paris?"

Owen raised an eyebrow. "You're a smart girl. You'll figure it out."

My cheeks were getting sore from smiling so widely.

"Text me the dates that you can arrive and depart, and I'll create an itinerary," he offered

I still just smiled in response. It was all too unreal.

"So it sounds like the concert was a success?" he changed the subject.

I nodded. "It was phenomenal. I'm really glad we went, even if the trip was obscenely expensive and resulted in a massive hangover and loads of makeup work."

"You'll have to show me your pictures later. And maybe, if you behave, I'll help you out with some of that makeup work."

I felt my lip twitch. "I thought you preferred it when I don't behave."

Owen's gaze deepened and I could see his breathing quicken.

He stood suddenly. "I believe my office hours are nearly over, so I should check if any other students are in need of my invaluable services."

I rose to my feet, lifting my backpack, while he opened his office door and peered out. I started towards the door just as he shut it, grabbed me, and pressed my back against the door.

"No one there," he murmured, as I enveloped him with a kiss.

OWEN

Bridget came over as planned Thursday evening, and even though neither of us behaved, I still helped her with her makeup work. We ordered Chinese rather than pizza this time, and instead of staying the night, she left at eleven, claiming she needed to catch up on sleep.

I had hoped she'd sleep over again, but I had to admit there was something to be said about her always leaving me wanting more.

The next morning, I was reaching to turn my phone to silent before class when I saw a text from Bridget.

"Your bed beats the cold dorm with 19 other girls any day," it read.

I felt my face flush as I put the phone away.

As usual, I didn't see Bridget Friday or Saturday, but on Sunday afternoon she called.

I couldn't help but smile as I answered. We went through the basic phone pleasantries, without her saying why she was calling, and then she asked what I'd been up to today.

"I went for a run, and then met a friend for lunch."

"What did you wear on the run?"

I frowned at the odd question. "Pants and a long sleeve tech shirt."

"Hmm. And this lunch, was it a date?"

"Sure. My date's name is Brian."

Now she laughed.

"So…what's going on with you?"

She sighed wistfully. "Nothing. Got my nails done this morning and then did homework. I keep getting distracted."

"By…?"

"You."

"But I haven't interrupted you once today."

"I know. Why is that? I could use a few interruptions."

She was definitely trying to hint at something, but I hadn't yet figured out what.

"I keep thinking about how you owe me a shower, but I suppose you already showered after your run. And now you're all clean."

Now I grinned. "I might get dirty again. In fact, if you have some free time, we could get dirty together, and then we could get around to that shower you were wanting."

"I thought you'd never ask. When should I come over?"

"As soon as you can."

Bridget arrived in under a half hour. She brought her backpack again, apparently thinking she might do some homework, but I kept her otherwise occupied until well after dinner.

BRIDGET

I was quickly becoming addicted to Owen. After my Sunday booty call, I forced myself to refrain from contacting him Monday. But seeing him in class Tuesday, looking all sexy and professional, was sure to drive me wild. Unfortunately, I barely got into the classroom door before being accosted by a different guy.

Jack casually slung his arm around my waist right as we hit the classroom door. "You know you want to come tonight," he insisted.

"Yeah, we'll see," I murmured, anxious for him to move his arm before Owen noticed.

Jack groaned loudly. "Those are very different answers, Bridg. Which is it—yeah or we'll see?"

We reached my usual seat and I shifted out of my backpack, conveniently forcing his arm off at the same time. I glanced to the front of the classroom, hopeful, but found Owen glaring back. Jack, thankfully, was oblivious.

"I'm not letting you sit down till you agree to come," Jack said, standing uncomfortably close. "If it's lame you can leave early."

By this point, I half expected to see steam shooting out of

Owen's ears, but instead, he had pulled his phone out of his bag.

"Bridget?" Jack repeated.

I smiled at him. "Yeah, sounds fun. I'll be there." It wasn't like I had other plans.

Besides, it would help keep things with Owen secret. So far, Stella hadn't questioned my absences. I'd always been social and spent a lot of time out and about, so I wasn't actually gone more than usual as of late. The difference was that lately, I was always with the same person. If I started skipping the sort of activity Stella knew I liked, like parties with cute baseball playing guys, that would surely raise suspicion.

"Awesome. Nine o'clock, alright?"

I nodded, and sat down, right as my phone buzzed. It was a text from Owen. "If you're trying to make me jealous, pick a better time," it said.

I gazed to the front of the classroom where Owen was looking right at me and shook my head. "Not trying to make u jealous," I replied.

Owen casually eyed his phone, shuffled some papers unnecessarily, and replied, "Then don't make dates with your new boyfriend in my classroom."

Before I could reply, Owen asked the class to quiet down and said we'd get started. I knew his class, like all others in the university, had a strict no-phone policy during class, meaning they were supposed to be put away and off during class, but I wondered if texts to the professor were an exception to the rule.

Owen asked the class to pass forward their homework assignments, so I seized the opportunity. Being in the front row, I dawdled at retrieving my own paper, so that by the time the rest of the students behind me had passed theirs forward, I was forced to walk mine up to Owen's desk.

"He's just a friend," I said in an angry whisper as I dropped my paper on his desk. I'd spoken so softly that I couldn't be sure Owen heard me, until about ten minutes later, when he gave the class five minutes to complete an assignment from the book. As we all began working quietly, I saw Owen retrieve his phone again. He was subtle enough that if I hadn't been watching him closely, I wouldn't have even known he was texting.

I had silenced my phone, thankfully, because when I slid it out of my bag a moment later, sure enough there was another message from Owen. "Don't be naïve. Jack wants you- not as a friend. Guarantee you he will make a move on you tonight."

I initially dismissed Owen's response as that of a jealous would-be boyfriend, but then I considered whether he might be right. It wasn't like Jack and I had a longstanding friendship, and he had been a little physical with his interactions lately.

I finally wrote back, "Fine, be jealous. Or trust me. Your choice."

"Ms. Williams," Owen said aloud just as I sent the text. "Phone?"

I cringed, blushing as the entire class turned to stare at me. I shoved my phone back into my backpack. "Sorry," I mumbled. As soon as Owen turned his back, I grimaced and rolled my eyes.

I then turned to see Jack grinning at me, apparently impressed with my impudence. I looked back to my paper, wondering what I'd gotten myself into.

I ditched Jack that night, instead heading over to Owen's. He was grinning when he opened the door.

"Don't smile at me like that," I chastised as he shut the door behind me. Then, I got a good look at him. He was wearing a sleeveless undershirt and thin jogging pants. Damn he looked sexy. "Did I interrupt your workout?"

"I was lifting weights. Mostly finished though," he said. "So why can't I smile at you?"

I turned away, struggling to be mad when he was looking so good. "You were a jerk today in class. You know I wasn't actually flirting with Jack so you could've just ignored it."

Owen took a long slow drink of water. "You were flirting with Jack," he said, lowering his gaze. "But I know you don't mean anything by it, so I'm sorry. It just makes it hard for me to concentrate in class when I'm thinking about you like this instead of you like a student."

"Like what? How am I now?"

He smirked and tugged my purse off my shoulder. "All breathless and flushed, fidgeting with your jewelry."

I relaxed my thumb that had been twisting my ring around.

Owen slid my shirt further down my shoulder, tracing his fingers along the curve of my neck so lightly that it tickled, forcing my head to tilt towards his hand. "I like this shirt," he said, his voice deeper now.

I was wearing black leggings and an off-the-shoulder merlot-colored top. The shirt was stretchy and clingy, but the material didn't breathe well, so instead of layering it over a black tank top like I assume was intended, I just let my black bra strap show. Now, however, my bra was hanging loosely around my back since Owen had unfastened it while I was distracted. He slid the shirt up over my head then, causing the bra to fall to the floor too. Then he smiled mischievously.

"I thought you liked the shirt."

"I like it better on the floor," he replied. He then fingered the long silver chain that hung between my breasts, as though deep in thought. "This can stay on," he decided.

I had intended to chastise him more for his antics in class, but all I could think about was how good it would feel to have his tongue lap across every sensitive spot of my body. It was frustrating to already be this aroused when he hadn't even touched me yet.

"How come you're still dressed?" I asked. "Not fair."

Without breaking eye contact, he reached for the hem of his shirt, then quickly hoisted it over his head. He then tugged my leggings down to my ankles, delicately supporting me while I stepped out of them. He gazed at me still, his breathing faster now, the look in his eyes menacing and hungry. Suddenly, he reached for me, roughly massaging my breasts with his hands, then suckling one at a time. I groaned loudly at the sudden onslaught of pleasure.

"Don't move," he ordered. I heard him open his night-stand drawer and my heart pounded faster, knowing exactly what he'd be retrieving from there. He walked back to me, smiled devilishly, and raised an eyebrow. "Turn around."

I complied, eager to hear his reaction to the only remaining article of clothing I wore. It was a new black lacy panty where the lace covered just the top of my butt cheeks. Not quite a thong, but by far the most flattering and sexy cut in my opinion. Owen moaned, signaling his agreement.

He smoothed his hand over my butt, squeezing the flesh in his hands. "I really wouldn't have been able to concentrate if I'd known you looked like this under your clothes," he whispered, reaching his hands around to my breasts.

I arched my back, pressing my breasts harder into his hands while my head fell back towards him. He kissed the side of my neck hungrily and my hands reached for something to grope. He grabbed my hands and placed them on the table in front of me, then slowly tugged my panties down to my feet. He didn't let me step out of them, but instead nudged my legs slightly further apart and licked me once, right where I ached the most.

He stood up, and just as I started to wonder what he

would do next, I felt his firm cock positioned at my entrance. He held my hips and slowly pressed into me. I sighed with the pleasure and relief of him filling me. He pressed gently on my back, nudging me down against the table, thrusting quickly and fully each time. I was breathless and dizzy and felt the pressure mounting quickly. A moment later, he reached for my breasts again, fondling them expertly while guiding me up to standing.

His teeth grazed the side of my neck, and it was too much to handle. Between his moist tongue on my skin, his fingers rolling my pebbled nipples and his cock stretching me and hitting just the right spot with every thrust, I quickly felt myself reaching the peak of ecstasy. I cried out loudly as I came, causing his thrusts to speed up briefly until he too came with a loud moan.

He held me tightly for a moment, then slowly lowered me back to the table as he pulled out. "Am I forgiven now?" he whispered before walking away. I was too breathless to answer.

I dressed quickly before he returned. He frowned as he approached.

"I liked that view," he whined, although as he'd put on shorts, he was a total hypocrite.

"I should go," I said.

Owen frowned and reached for my hand. "You don't have to leave," he said, tugging me closer and kissing me on the mouth. I realized that was actually our first kiss of the day. Well, first on the lips anyway. We were both smiling by the time our lips broke apart.

"I'll let you get back to your workout," I said.

"I liked tonight's workout. I could use a similar one tomorrow night, say same time?"

I nearly agreed, then remembered I'd promised Stella I'd go to a frat party with her. Normally, I wasn't in to mid-week parties, but it was at Jerrod's house so she was definitely going, and it would help prevent her from becoming suspicious about my frequent absences from other social events lately.

"I can't. I have plans with Stella tomorrow night. Probably not this much fun though."

He laughed, then nodded and watched me go.

CHAPTER 12

OWEN

On Thursday morning, I awoke suddenly to the blaring of my alarm. I reached to shut it off, only to find the noise actually emanating from my cell phone. I rubbed my eyes and checked the caller ID before answering.

"Bridget? Are you okay? It's one o'clock in the morning."

There was loud music in the background and I almost concluded she had dialed me on accident when a man spoke.

"Uh, no dude. I'm not Bridget. But, um, there's a girl passed out on the couch here and this is her phone."

"What?" In an instant, I was wide awake. "Who is this?"

"Man, I just found her phone. Looked like you guys are tight so I thought I'd call you. If my girl were passed out drunk I'd want to know."

"Where is she?" I repeated, standing and flicking on a light to grab a pen in case I needed to write down an address. The guy named a fraternity that I knew how to get to and told me she was on the third floor in room 315.

I pulled on my jeans and zipped my coat up over the tee shirt I'd fallen asleep wearing. "Wait, you're sure she's just asleep? She's okay?"

"Yeah, man, she's breathing."

That reassured me, although the caller was clearly trashed so it probably shouldn't have been too comforting.

"Can you stay with her? Make sure no one touches her and that she's still okay until I get there?"

"Dude, this isn't even my room. I don't wanna start shit. You can come get her."

He hung up, and I swore under my breath and raced to the car. There was a faculty-only parking lot across the street from the house, so I didn't have to deal with that mess. I called Bridget as I pulled into a spot, praying she'd answer. It would be great if she could meet me outside and spare me the humiliation of having to trek through a frat house to find her, but mostly I wanted confirmation that she was okay. I knew she had a wild side, that she liked to have fun, but passing out at a frat house didn't sound like her.

I hung up the phone when it reached her voice mail and sped up. There was no one manning the door or collecting cover charges anymore, I supposed, because of the late hour. I was grateful for that, but still figured my chances of getting out of the house with Bridget without being spotted by any of my students were slim to none.

I paused as I entered, suddenly disoriented. The room was very dimly lit, packed with students, and it reeked of beer. The hip hop song blaring through the speakers was so loud that it vibrated throughout my body. When my eyes finally adjusted to the darkness, I spotted the staircase. I kept my head down as I made my way across the crowded room, wincing as beer splashed onto my coat.

Just as I reached the stairs, I noticed two girls dancing on a table to the right of the stairwell. Doing a double take, I confirmed one was Bridget. The relief at seeing her conscious and unharmed was instantaneous, but fleeting. Soon I was just pissed. How was she this irresponsible? What was she thinking?

I tried to get her attention, but she was in her own drunken world and her long hair hung in front of her face. She was barefoot, wearing skin tight black pants and a fitted sleeveless white top. Glow-in-the-dark bracelets lined both of her arms and she wore a matching necklace. She held a red solo cup in one hand and her other arm waved freely above her head as she swayed. I was momentarily distracted by how sexy she was up there, but then I noticed the half dozen or so other guys gawking at her, and my anger returned.

Suddenly, she spotted me. Her face lit up and she started towards me, completely forgetting she was on top of a table. I lunged forward and caught her just as she would've toppled over the edge.

"Hey! What are you doing here?" she slurred happily.

"Some guy called me from your phone saying you were passed out on a couch upstairs," I explained. "Where are your shoes?"

She gazed down to her feet and appeared genuinely surprised not to see them in shoes. I spotted a pair of designer high heels near the wall and grabbed them.

"Are these yours?"

She nodded.

"Okay, come on," I said, motioning to the door. We could wait until she was outside to put on her shoes.

"Wait, so who called you?" she had to shout over the music.

"I don't know. Some guy had your phone."

She frowned. "That's weird. I gave it to Stella to hold onto."

I froze in my tracks and swore under my breath. "Stella has your phone?"

"I thought she did."

I cursed again, wishing I could leave now without being spotted by anyone and not be wracked with guilt all night. But I knew I couldn't just leave her best friend unconscious in a frat house, so I led Bridget up the stairs. We found room 315 easily and the door was ajar. Bridget pushed it open.

"Yep, there's Stella," she said. "And here's my phone."

I rolled my eyes, crouching down and shaking the girl's arm. She winced and shook her head, which I suppose was a good sign. I had no clue how to get two drunk girls out of a fraternity without attracting attention though. I sat back on my heels to think and noticed Bridget tapping away on her phone.

"What are you doing?" I snapped, assuming she was tweeting about the party or some immature shit like that.

"Texting her boyfriend," she said, oblivious to my harsh tone. "This is his house."

I considered that for a moment. "Wait, Jerrod? My student, Jerrod?" I stood quickly. "I can't be here, Bridget. I can't explain that."

She shrugged, staggering to the side drunkenly. "It's fine, you go. I can get a ride home after he comes up to get Stella."

No part of me trusted her ability to get herself safely home in this condition, but I also wasn't about to sit around and wait for a student to find me alone in a fraternity room with two intoxicated girls.

"I'm not leaving you, Bridget. I'm going to my car now, though, and don't tell anyone I was here. As soon as Jerrod is here and you're sure your friend is okay, come out and find me and I'll drive you home. Do you understand?"

She nodded, but she'd started swaying to the music again, which was infuriating.

"If I call, you answer right away, okay?"

Bridget saluted me like a drunken sailor. I gritted my teeth, but ducked my head and scurried out of the fraternity as fast as I could.

I was breathing hard and my pulse was racing by the time I got to my car. I didn't think anyone had noticed me, but I couldn't say for sure. I was so angry that my fists were shaking. I always considered myself a level-headed guy, but everything about tonight just pissed me off. I glanced at my phone, wondering where Bridget was and what was taking her so long, only to realize that a mere four minutes had passed. I'd give her a full ten minutes before calling. And at that point, if she didn't answer, maybe I'd just call the cops on the whole thing rather than risk going back in again.

I couldn't believe Bridget would be so irresponsible. She could've gotten alcohol poisoning. Her friend still could have it. Jesus, she could've been gang raped, or drugged, or locked in a cellar of some creepy guy. And what was her plan to get home in the first place? Had she just intended to pass out on Jerrod's floor? To carpool in to class with him the next morning?

I startled at a sudden noise and saw Bridget opening the car door. I sighed with relief, then rolled my eyes as she struggled to get in and buckle herself.

"Is Stella okay?"

"She's fine," she said. "She was awake and making out with Jerrod when I left." She rolled down the window and tilted her head towards it.

I winced at that image. "Bridget, she was really drunk. You don't think he'll take advantage of her?"

Bridget snickered. "He's not a complete asshole, you know. And anything he'd do to her drunk she'd agree to when sober anyway, so I'm not worried. It's not like he's gonna loan her out to his friends for a turn. And she's on the pill anyway."

I suddenly felt sorry for the fathers of every teenage girl. I wanted to shake Bridget, to scream at her how stupid all of this was, but I knew it was pointless. She probably wouldn't even remember it happening by tomorrow. So instead I drove, pulling up to her sorority, and unfastening her belt.

"Drink some water. I'll call you tomorrow," I said, and then I watched as she stumbled into the building.

* * *

THAT AFTERNOON, I had just finished grading a short essay when there was a tap on my door. Because it was my office hours, the door was open, but most students waited to be invited in regardless.

"Come in," I said, flipping the stack of essays face down before glancing up.

It was Bridget. She stepped inside, shut the door behind her, then sat.

I stood and immediately opened the blinds over my door. Usually I left them shut when meeting with a student to offer the student some privacy, but in light of the previous night, I didn't want to risk anyone questioning what I was doing alone in my office with Bridget.

"You weren't in class," I said, stating the obvious as I returned to my desk. Jerrod had not appeared either, thought I figured Bridget already knew that too.

She slid her wide-rimmed black designer sunglasses off of her face and arranged them on top of her head. Her dark brown hair was pulled into a messy bun that she probably thought was unattractive but was actually incredibly sexy and reminded me of the way she looked after sex, when she wasn't trying so hard to be perfect. She was wearing some form of sweatpants or leggings that similarly looked casual and comfortable but framed her perky butt perfectly. Her hoodie was partway unzipped, so I could see a fitted ribbed tank top beneath it, clinging to her boobs. Her makeup was minimal and her jewelry nonexistent.

"You look like shit," I said. She didn't, of course, but I could tell she felt crappy.

"Gee thanks."

"How's Stella?"

"Still sleeping." She paused and then, correctly interpreting my expression, added, "she's not dead. I checked. And she's had some water."

"Is that why you missed class?"

Bridget shook her head. "I overslept."

I suppressed an eye roll. "Yeah, you were out pretty late. Especially for a Wednesday."

"I thought you would call today."

I was surprised she even remembered that. "I would've, later. I've been working. Not all of us can just take the day off to nurse a hangover."

She gazed to the window. "I'm really sorry about last night. I should have told you where I was going and I shouldn't have left my purse with Stella. I didn't mean for you to have to come out in the middle of the night to get us."

"It's not even about that. I was really worried about you, Bridget. I shouldn't have to wonder if you're out getting trashed at fraternity houses when we aren't together. You or your friend could've gotten alcohol poisoning or raped. And we could have been caught."

She didn't answer.

I flung my hands up. "Do you know how many people saw me there last night? If any one of those people knows who I am, it's going to be really hard to explain what I was doing there. And what about the guy who used your phone to call me? He obviously read enough of our texts to know to call me, so he clearly knows we're involved. I could lose my job over this, Bridget."

"I know that, Owen. And I said I'm sorry. Look," she held her cell phone out, showing me the contact information for someone named Enzo.

I frowned.

"That's you. I don't have you in my phone by your real name. So unless that guy recognized your voice, he's not an issue."

I smiled slightly at the pseudonym she'd chosen. "Enzo?"

She shrugged. "I remembered your story about your first Italian professor calling you that. It seemed appropriate."

I turned to the door, thankful no one else had showed up for office hours yet. It was a relief knowing my name wasn't in her phone, especially in light of some of the things we'd texted to each other, but that didn't really solve the problem. I figured it was a slim chance that anyone at the party recognized me and was sober enough to notice I was leaving with an undergraduate, but still…I'd be on pins and needles for at least the next week waiting to hear if anyone said anything.

"I get it, Owen. I know I screwed up, and I'm sorry."

I could tell from the look on her face that she meant what she was saying, but she clearly didn't understand how serious this was. I felt like an asshole doing this when she was clearly hungover, but obviously we'd both known this couldn't last forever.

"Bridget, I'm trying to focus on my career now and I need to take that seriously. You just want to have fun. You have no concept of responsibility."

Her eyes narrowed. "Are you fucking kidding me?"

"I can't spend my nights in some random stuffy house doing shots and dancing. I don't want to, anyway. I'm not twenty-one anymore."

She rolled her eyes now. "Yeah, well I am, and sometimes I want to have fun. Sometimes I don't want to sit around and watch you grade papers while all my friends are out partying. And I get why you're pissed about last night, and that won't happen again. But I can't handle you being a dick every time I want to act my age."

"I know," I agreed. "It's not fair to you or me. We're just in two different places in our lives. We knew from the start this wasn't going to be easy. It was fun while it lasted, but I think it's time we cut our losses and stop fooling around."

"Fooling around?" she repeated.

The look in her eyes was heartbreaking. "Bridget, you know what I mean."

She blew out a sigh. "Yeah, I guess I do. I just, well, that wasn't how I thought of what we've been doing."

I tried to think of something else to say, but I knew I had to let it go. This was for the best, for both of us. Anything else I said now would just confuse things further. I glanced to the door and saw another student was waiting to speak with me.

"You should go," I finally said. "I'll see you in class Tuesday."

She hesitated, her hand clenched so tightly around her water bottle that I worried she was about to throw it at my head. Instead, she walked slowly towards the door.

"You are just like everyone else," she said softly. "You only want me when I'm perfect."

Before I could answer, she tugged open the door. She stared straight at the guy waiting to see me next and mumbled, "Good luck. Hope you didn't oversleep, too. He's not in a forgiving mood."

CHAPTER 13

BRIDGET

I ditched the rest of my classes that week, opting instead to alternate between napping and crying. Stella woke by mid-afternoon, and knowing I'd need some explanation of my moodiness, and of how I got home, I told her I'd almost hooked up with a guy in the frat before I realized he was a total jerk and made him drive me home.

We treated ourselves to manicures, went to our favorite diner for a greasy 5PM dinner, then spent the evening experimenting with various pudding shot recipes and watching old Kevin Bacon movies. It was just distracting enough to take my mind off Owen, but as I switched off my light for bed, I saw a text.

It was from Owen, and it read, "You are perfect, no matter what you do. Anyone who says otherwise is an idiot. And it wasn't just fooling around for me either. I don't know why I said that. I guess I was angry. But I'm no good for you. You should be with someone who makes you happy and lets you be yourself. Sorry for everything."

I inhaled deeply, determined not to cry, but by the time I exhaled, I was sobbing.

* * *

I ATTENDED all of my classes Monday and Tuesday, except Owen's. I still couldn't stomach the thought of seeing him again. I assumed he'd notice my absence and I liked to think he'd wonder where I was, but I hadn't expected a text the instant class ended.

"You missed class again. Are you okay?" it read.

"Fine. As per the attendance policy, I still have one allotted absence left, right?" I replied.

He took his time writing back, but eventually did, curtly noting I was correct about the policy and "highly" recommending I attend Thursday. I assumed that meant there was going to be a quiz.

As much as I wanted to prove him right about me and show him just how irresponsible I could be, I couldn't bring myself to skip a quiz. Instead, I'd just make him jealous. The brown had been growing out of my hair for weeks, so I had it dyed back to my natural fiery red. I paired my sexiest skinny jeans with an emerald green top, the exact color of my eyes. The top was perfect though, since it coordinated with my new hair and appeared casual enough, but was actually fairly low cut and always attracted all the wrong kinds of attention.

I waited way down the hall from class so as not to arrive early. Right before class started, Eric, the well-known class slacker and go-to guy for pot and ecstasy on campus, walked past me. Seeing him gave me a great idea, even more effective than arriving slightly late to class.

"Eric!" I called after him.

He turned, gave me a suggestive once over, and grinned.

"Hey, totally random but do you have any cash?"

He raised a brow.

"I need to borrow like three dollars. I can pay you back Tuesday."

Eric shrugged. "Yeah, sure." He rummaged around in his pocket and handed me the money.

"Thank you," I said, smiling sweetly. We headed into class together, making small talk. "I'm really not in the mood for this today," I said to him right as we passed Owen's desk. I was acutely aware of Owen turning in my direction, but neither of us made a big deal about it.

I sat near the front, in my normal spot, but made a big show out of rummaging around in my bag. I pulled out the money Eric had loaned me and folded it up so it looked like more. Then I walked to the back of the class where Eric was sitting.

I held the money up then tucked it into Eric's notebook, bending over to whisper. "So turns out I am a total spaz and had the money in my backpack, but thanks anyway," I said.

"No problem," Eric replied, grinning now at what I assume had to be a fabulous view down my shirt.

I walked back to my desk, feeling ridiculously victorious and immature as I caught Owen's wide-eyed stare. Being the bad girl was fun, I decided. I might have to do it more often.

Owen didn't call on me during class, and he didn't give us a quiz, but he did explain our next essay assignment.

The moment class was over, I made a beeline for Jack's desk. Since my friendship with him had made Owen jealous before, I figured it couldn't hurt to flaunt that now.

"Hey," Jack greeted me, taking his time rising out of his seat.

"Hey yourself," I replied. "Stella and I are looking for a party this weekend. Got any leads?"

Jack grinned. "Oh yeah. Nice hair, by the way," he said, tugging a few strands.

"Thank you," I said, smiling sweetly. We walked out together, Jack listing me the possible options for weekend fun.

* * *

ON TUESDAY, I walked into class with Eric again, keeping my sunglasses over my eyes until after I slid into my seat. I hadn't consumed even a sip of alcohol on Monday, but I did my best to pretend to be hungover.

When class ended, I started back towards Eric's desk, but Owen called me before I got there.

"Ms. Williams, a moment," he said.

I rolled my eyes dramatically before turning to face him and nodding complacently. I silently waited as he packed up his messenger bag, then followed him to his office one floor up.

"Have a seat," he said, shutting the door.

I complied, trying not to remember what had happened the last time I was in that very seat.

He stared at me for a moment before speaking. "Are you hungover?" he finally asked.

I stared back expressionless.

"Drunk?"

"No!" I replied. Even though I had thought I wanted him to reach that conclusion, I was now insulted.

He appeared relieved at my reaction, but persisted regardless. "Then what's going on? You're buying drugs off of Eric and going to parties with Jack?"

I rolled my eyes. "I'm twenty-one. I'm acting my age."

"Bridget, come on. This isn't you."

"Apparently it is. I took a short break from my normal persona and now I'm back to being a dumb party girl."

Owen picked a pencil up off his desk and tapped it rapidly against the wood. He started to speak several times and then stopped himself. Finally, he said, "I feel like all of this is my fault. I'm worried about you, Bridget."

"It's not your fault that I have no concept of responsibility."

His face fell. "Bridg, I'm sorry. I didn't mean that. I was mad."

I shrugged. "Don't worry about it. I'm fine."

"You don't seem fine."

"Why do you care?"

"Because I do," he replied.

"Now I'm just confused on the post-fooling around etiquette."

Owen walked around to the front of his desk and leaned against it. "You know it wasn't like that, Bridget."

I gazed down at my feet, unable to look at him without simultaneously wanting to strangle him and lick him. "I really don't, Owen. I know what I felt, and I thought I knew what you felt, but apparently I was all wrong. I was just another student to you all along."

"Bridget you know that isn't true. There was no other student that I…" he shook his head, flustered. "You weren't just another student to me. You have to know I care about you. It's killing me watching you do this to yourself."

"I'm not your responsibility any more, Owen."

He nodded.

"Is that all?" I needed to get out of his office before I burst into tears.

Owen tilted his head towards the ceiling. "I don't know. I feel awful about all of this. I shouldn't have gotten involved with you and I was trying to do the right thing last week. I didn't mean to hurt you."

I bit the inside of my lip.

"Are you sure you're okay?" he asked.

I waved my hand into the air. "No, I'm really not. But I'm not on drugs and I'm not drinking too much or partying all the time, so you don't need to worry. I'll be fine eventually." I paused and wiped my eyes. "Right now, I just miss you, okay? And I'm feeling a little hurt because I thought you had real feelings for me until you told me it was just sex and made me feel like an immature brat."

"I did have real feelings for you, Bridget. I still do, but I'm not the right man for you. You could do so much better."

"You want me to be with someone else?"

"No," he said instantly. "It makes me sick seeing you even talking with other guys. But it isn't fair to you that I can't take you out in public. There's so many guys your own age."

"You're not that much older."

"You know it's not just the age difference," he reminded me.

I had no response for that.

He dropped his head down. "I miss you, too," he said finally. "This really sucks."

"It doesn't have to," I said.

He didn't reply, so I stood, defeated.

But before I could turn away, he reached for my hands. "If we don't say goodbye now, we're just going to be back in this same position in a few weeks," he said.

I shrugged, dizzy from the feeling of his hands wrapped around mine. "I'm okay with that."

"I didn't mean to be such a jerk last weekend. I was so scared when that guy called me. I pictured all sorts of bad things happening to you."

"I'm sorry. I won't let that happen again. I'm really not like that normally."

"I know that," he said.

"You really missed me?"

He laughed. "Yes. So much."

"I'm okay with not going out in public with you. No one will find out."

Owen's eyes lit up, but still he hesitated. "You deserve more."

"I don't want more."

He grinned, tugging slightly on my hands to pull me closer. His eyes lingered on mine much longer than my patience could tolerate. We were close enough for me to smell his aftershave and to feel his breath on my forehead. I had to touch him. I rose to my toes tentatively, letting him tilt his head downward to bridge the remaining two-inch gap between us.

He moaned softly into my mouth as we made contact, and I responded in kind. I pulled my hand free from his so I could touch his hair. I knew girls tended to act like a guy's hair isn't a big deal, but Owen had nice hair. It was the ideal length—just long enough to run my fingers through it or tug on it but not so long that it got crazy on windy, rainy or humid days. It was thick and soft, and the shade of sand just before the tide rises.

Owen groaned and pulled back abruptly. "We can't do this here," he whispered, his lips grazing my ear.

I nodded reluctantly, refraining from reminding him we had done that there before.

"Call me later?" I asked.

He frowned. "Come over tonight. Unless you have plans with Jack?"

I laughed. "Seven o'clock good?"

He nodded, so I turned to leave.

"I love the hair," he said.

I ran my hand along the back of my hair, having temporarily forgotten about the dramatic color change. "I did it for you," I admitted.

"You play dirty," he said, his eyes dark with desire.

"Oh, I plan to," I teased, winking as I left his office.

OWEN

When Bridget came over that night, I hadn't known what to expect. I thought we might talk first, or that it might be awkward, but instead we were kissing the moment the door shut. A few minutes later, we were making love in my bed. It was more tender and slower than our usual, but equally—if not more—satisfying.

Afterwards, we were lying in bed when I remembered something she'd said earlier. It had bothered me a lot. "Bridg, what did you mean when you said I was just like everyone else who only liked you when you're perfect?"

"Nothing. I was upset."

"Yeah, but you could have said anything. Why that?"

"Well, it fit. I screwed up, and at the first sign I wasn't perfect, you dumped me. I'd always worried I wasn't good enough for you, and that just reinforced my fear."

Her words cut through me like a knife. "Jesus. I'm sorry Bridget. That wasn't how I was thinking, though. I just thought it was a sign, a reminder that we don't make sense together. I never for a moment thought *you* weren't good enough for *me*."

She sighed.

"You said everyone, though. Who else makes you feel that way?"

I couldn't fathom someone actually treating her like she

wasn't perfect, but it killed me to think she ever even felt less than perfect.

"Patrick," she said.

"Your ex?"

"Yep."

I didn't press for details, and I hoped that was the end of the list, but it wasn't.

"Both of my serious high school boyfriends. Chris dumped me when I didn't make the cheerleading squad, saying it just wasn't right for the captain of the football team to go out with a girl who wasn't a cheerleader. And Dave, well I broke up with him, but he was always ranting about how I was too short."

She sighed, but then continued. "And then there's my dad. He's my number one fan and best friend, always buying me stuff and bragging about me to people, but then the second I would screw up and cut class or miss curfew or get caught smoking with a boy, he'd shut me out completely. For weeks, it was like I just didn't exist. Then my mom, well she's never outright criticized anything, but she always makes these comments about how I shouldn't cut my hair or I won't be as pretty, and I better not eat so many carbs or boys won't like me, and I shouldn't double major because what's the point when I'm not the smart one."

"She said you're not the smart one?" I couldn't even believe my ears.

"Well, maybe not in those words, but she implies it all the time. I'm pretty sure she thinks a college degree is a total waste on me and that the only reason I'm here is to meet a guy who can pay for my beauty treatments."

I squeezed her tighter. "She's crazy. All of them are. No one is perfect, but you're pretty damn close. And you could shave your head and gain fifty pounds and everyone would still flock to you because you're just so magnetic."

She sighed and burrowed further against my arm.

I interpreted that as the end of the discussion. I scooted out from under her and kissed her head before crouching down by her feet. "I think you're perfect from your head to your toes," I said, kissing the tip of her toe.

Bridget giggled and curled her toes in. "I cannot believe you just kissed my toe. Ewww."

Since she had clearly showered immediately before coming to my apartment, I didn't take her disgust as serious protest, but rather a challenge. I gripped her calf and raised her foot to my face, locking eyes with her as I licked each of her toes. Bridget writhed around on the bed, clearly ticklish.

"The first time I saw you, you were wearing the most ridiculous shoes ever."

"I was not!" she exclaimed.

"You were too. Those silver strappy ones? You could barely walk."

"Those are Manolos. It doesn't matter if you can walk when your feet are wrapped in a gorgeous one of a kind piece of art!"

I laughed, pleased that she could still surprise me, as I had clearly underestimated her love of shoes. "My point is, I saw those shoes, and I saw how pretty you were, and I assumed you were shallow and self-absorbed."

"Sounds accurate," she said, thrusting her fingers into my hair as I worked my way up her calves.

"It is not accurate! Do you remember the first thing you did on that day?"

"Checked out my hot new professor?"

"No, you went and struck up a conversation with the dorky guy in the corner."

Bridget started laughing. "Did you just call a student a dork?"

Guilty as charged, I didn't answer.

"Anyways I was only talking to him because we both liked the Cubs."

So she did remember. "You were not. Any of the other guys in that class would've gladly discussed baseball with you, but you sought out Mark solely because he was all alone."

"Be the sunshine," she said.

"What?" I lifted my head up from her thigh.

Bridget sighed. "It's something my grandma used to say. When the sun isn't shining, be the sunshine. She used to tell me I had the power to walk into a room and cheer anyone up."

"You still do," I said. "I wish you saw in yourself what everyone else sees."

I traced my tongue higher along her thigh and felt her breathing quicken. She clenched her hands into my shoulders, her lower body writhing against my mouth. Probably the time for serious discussion had ended.

CHAPTER 14

OWEN

I didn't see Bridget as much over the next week due to midterms. For all of her claims that she didn't care about classes, she always did study when it mattered. When her last test was done and she came over, we spent more than our usual time in bed.

I'd been meaning to tell to her about something, but forgot until she already had her purse in hand and was preparing to leave.

"Wait. Can we talk for a second?"

Bridget glanced up, alarmed.

"Nothing bad." I handed her the paper.

She skimmed through it quickly. "This looks like info about a scholarship for students double majoring in Italian and French."

I nodded. "But it's not exactly a scholarship. It's a flat out cash award you can use towards travel or grad school."

"I'm not a double major. Why are you showing this to me?"

"You could be. There's so few at our university who double major in both French and Italian that you'd be almost guaranteed to win."

"I only have one year left. That's not enough time to add a major."

"It is, though. This summer you'll get more than enough credits to finish the Italian minor. You can count your linguistics class and one of your French classes towards your Italian major and then one of your Italian classes can count towards the French major. So you can drop one French class you'd planned to take and add two Italian classes each semester next year and you'll have enough for both majors."

She frowned.

"You could drop bowling. There is room in your schedule."

"You looked at my schedule?"

I shrugged. I had snooped, yes. But for a legit educational purpose.

"That sounds really complicated."

"It isn't. I just want you to think about it. If there's any chance you might be interested in continuing Italian, you should do it. You can easily add Italian classes into your fall schedule at this point, and if you decide you don't want them later, you could drop them again."

"What about…" she hesitated, raising an eyebrow. "Won't it be hard guaranteeing I don't end up in your classes?"

"No. I know what classes I'm teaching in the fall already, so just don't sign up for those and it's all good. Professor Mancini teaches two you'd love."

She still looked skeptical.

"Just tell me you'll think about it, okay?"

She nodded and we kissed. We were each heading to our

respective hometowns for spring break, so we wouldn't see each other for a week.

BRIDGET

Normally I would've protested my mom insisting I spend spring break at home rather than somewhere along the Gulf Coast with friends, but since I was leaving for Europe in six weeks, I figured I owed her some face time. It wasn't all bad, anyway. My dad took me to Chicago to see the Cubs' home opener, and my mom treated me to a new wardrobe for Italy.

Owen and I texted several times each day, sharing random tidbits about our families but mostly focusing on our upcoming trip. At night, we'd talk for hours after my parents were asleep. It was comforting to know that Owen still enjoyed my company when we weren't in bed. I knew he hadn't meant the comment about us just fooling around, but ever since then I'd noticed I still wasn't completely confident that he was interested in me as more than a sexual partner.

"You were up late last night," my mom said suddenly, cutting into my thoughts.

I panicked, hoping she hadn't overheard too much of my conversation. "Oh, well, I was just talking with Stella."

She nodded. "Is that who you're texting all the time, too?"

"Yep," I lied without hesitation.

"Too bad. I thought maybe you were seeing someone new. Or maybe that you'd rekindled things with Patrick?" Her tone was so hopeful that I just knew she was already picturing my wedding dress.

"Patrick is an asshole, Mom. I will never go out with him again."

She placed the dish she was drying on the counter and gazed up at me, surprised. It took her a moment to regain her composure. "Oh. Well, okay then. I hadn't realized..." She

LIZA MALLOY

resumed drying dishes in silence before changing topics. "So you said there's a professor from your school headed to Italy with the same program?"

My stomach clenched. "Yes. Professor Chambers. I had him both semesters this year. He has taught at the academy in Florence in previous summers, so I think it'll be good to have someone familiar with it to help me get my bearings."

This seemed to comfort my mom, and she let the topic drop.

OWEN

Olivia and I went out for pizza and drinks the last night I was in town. Her husband was working late, so it was just the two of us. We blew through the preliminaries quickly, having done a decent job of keeping in touch since Christmas via text. Then, Olivia quickly launched into the stuff she really wanted to know.

"When are you going to settle down and get married?" she asked.

"Gee Mom, I don't know."

She elbowed me, scowling. "Yeah, yeah. It's just that I always thought we'd be going through all these phases together, or at least relatively close in time. But I'm already married and you're still sleeping with every girl you meet, and now Dave and I are ready to start a family, and…"

"Whoa whoa whoa," I interrupted, turning to her. "You're not… are you pregnant?"

"No, not yet. But I'd like to be, maybe in the next year or so."

I exhaled the breath I'd been inadvertently holding. We both paused and sipped our drinks. "I'm not sleeping with every girl I meet."

She smiled. "Well, maybe you'll meet someone in Italy."

I fiddled with my watch nervously.

Olivia's eyes widened. "What? I know that look. You're not telling me something."

"I've been seeing someone, pretty much the whole semester," I said, glancing around furtively as though expecting to find spies in her living room.

"What?" My sister looked angry.

"We aren't telling people yet. I couldn't say anything."

She rolled her eyes dramatically. "What, are you like a finalist on the Bachelorette or something? Of course you can tell me. You can always tell me." She shook her head again. "All semester?"

I nodded reluctantly.

"Well, who is it? Have I met her? Show me a picture!"

I braced myself for a violent outburst as I answered. "I can't."

"Owen, you are being ridiculous. I'm not going to tell anyone. You know that. And telling me doesn't even count as telling someone. We're twins. It's like doctor-patient confidentiality. Or attorney-client privilege."

I considered this for a moment before relenting. "You met her once."

Olivia's jaw dropped. "I knew it!"

"What? You knew nothing! You still don't know."

She shook her head. "Yes, I do. It's that girl, right? The one you were studying with before your dissertation."

Wow. I had to admit her twin-sense was pretty impressive. I swallowed before reminding Olivia of the reason this was all so top secret. "Yes. That's her. My student."

"Former student," she said.

I shook my head. "Afraid not."

Olivia sighed.

"Don't look at me like that. I already know everything

you're thinking, and I've already thought about all the reasons it's a bad idea, and I just can't walk away."

"Is the girl going to Italy with you?"

"Her name is Bridget, and she's a woman, not a girl. She's twenty-one." I ignored my sister's scoff. "And yes, she'll be there."

"As your student?"

"As *a* student, yes. But it's different over there, you know? And when we get back, she won't be my student anymore so we can have a normal relationship then."

Olivia's eyes were filled with disappointment. "Owen, I just want you to be happy."

"I know, and I am. Happier than I ever was with Laura. Bridget is just so…"

"Gorgeous," Olivia supplied.

"I was going to say refreshing, but yes, she is gorgeous. But she's also smart and funny and vibrant. She's so full of life and energetic."

"Of course she's energetic. She's twenty-one!"

I laughed despite myself. "I'm around twenty-somethings all day and I assure you Bridget is different. She's different from anyone I've ever met."

She finished her drink and patted my knee. "Well, I'm glad you're happy. And when this all blows up in your face, there are lots of single women from Dave's work that I can fix you up with."

I knew she was teasing, but I also couldn't shake the ominous feeling that Olivia was always right.

BRIDGET

When I returned to school, I focused fully on final exams and Italy. Owen had hammered out the final details of our travels for before the summer classes began. I took the plunge and applied for the award Owen recommended, and I made the necessary adjustments to my first semester schedule to accommodate the double major. I was too wussy to officially declare the second major, but I could do that in the fall.

The two weeks of finals were a blur, and before I knew it, I was spending my last night in the U.S. with Owen. Well, I'd be in the country for a couple more weeks, but it was the last time we'd be together before Europe. I was nervous about the trip—the long flight, the foreign culture, the classes…but I was especially anxious about how the whole experience would affect us as a couple.

Things with Owen had been good. Really good, actually. We were so in sync, so happy, and everything just felt right. But I'd felt that way before, and then he'd dumped me. I wasn't sure I could handle being suddenly rejected in a foreign country with no comfort foods or best friend to pull me through it.

Owen seemed to sense my unease that night, as he was definitely holding me tighter and longer than normal. I didn't want to discuss my insecurities though, since I suspected that would just make me feel sillier, so I raised a different topic instead.

"I was making a list of things to pack and trying to figure out what I could just buy once I arrived, and I thought you may have some insight on a few things," I began.

"You will find every beauty and hair product made in Florence," he immediately replied. "And jewelry. And shoes."

I laughed, certain based on his tone that he was envisioning me packing four suitcases of designer crap.

"Good to know, but I was specifically curious about condoms."

He raised an eyebrow. "I figured I would pack some of those, but they do sell them there as well. You worried we'll run out?"

I hesitated. "I thought maybe we should talk about whether we need to pack them at all."

His eyes widened and I laughed, realizing he thought I was suggesting abstinence.

"I'm on the pill," I said. "Birth control."

Owen's face relaxed. "Oh. Since when?"

I considered lying, but then went with the truth. "The whole time we've been together."

He sat upright. "And you're just now telling me?"

"It didn't seem like a big deal to use condoms," I replied. "And I wasn't sure about…well, birth control only prevents pregnancy and doesn't protect against anything else. I wanted to make sure we didn't need to be concerned about anything else before we stopped using them. And…" I hesitated again. "I wasn't sure if either of us were still sleeping with other people."

Owen frowned. "Either of us? You mean me?"

I shrugged. "Well, I know I haven't been with anyone else since we became involved."

Owen shook his head. "Me neither. Did you honestly think I was sleeping with other people?"

I sighed. I had hoped he wasn't, but I was too scared to assume. It was a lot easier to avoid getting hurt if I didn't jump to conclusions about our exclusivity.

"Bridget, I have no interest in sleeping with anyone else, here or in Italy. And I'm clean, so if you're comfortable without condoms then I am all in favor of freeing up some luggage space."

I nodded and let him kiss me until I forgot what I was so stressed about.

CHAPTER 15

OWEN

Two weeks before Bridget was scheduled to fly into Paris, I arrived in Italy. I settled into the apartment where I'd spend the greater part of the next fifteen weeks, a small but charming studio a short walk from campus, and I busied myself with lesson plans and learning the ways of the university. Being back in Italy—and knowing I had an entire summer there—was exhilarating. I was eager to travel, but equally excited to fully immerse myself in the local Firenze culture.

I traveled to France to meet Bridget as planned, but felt reluctant, which I hadn't anticipated. I knew we'd have a wonderful time exploring France together, but what would happen when we returned to Italy? She was never needy or clingy back home, but in a foreign country with no family and no friends aside from me, Bridget might not be her typical independent self.

My concerns were fleeting, though, and I forgot them

altogether once I saw her, looking surprisingly refreshed and put together for just having endured an international flight. Watching her take in all the sights in France was mesmerizing. Everything she encountered, she loved. She was fascinated by my stories about the architecture, stuffed herself shamelessly with the local delicacies, and embraced each adventure with the enthusiasm and wonder of a child seeing Disney World for the first time.

On our last day in France, we lingered at a café in Nice, having worked our way closer and closer to the Italian border over the course of the week. That afternoon, we would travel by train to Florence, a seven hour trip after factoring in switching trains, and Bridget would stay at my apartment that night. She'd arranged for her own room on campus, but since we would arrive so late at night, it made more sense for her to stay with me and get settled into her own place first thing in the morning.

"I'm going to miss having you in my bed every night," I admitted.

She grinned. "I'm going to miss holding your hand in public."

I would miss that, too. I had carefully read and re-read the rules of the program and saw nothing on the Italian side that prevented me from engaging in a romantic relationship with a participant in the program. I noted from the paperwork that Bridget received, however, that our local university claimed that all of our local rules applied while she was a student with the program. So, I didn't think we could safely flaunt our relationship, which would mean no kissing in public, something I'd definitely miss. But we could spend more time together openly in Italy. I wasn't actually her professor in the program, but as the only people from our campus there for the program, no one would question if we were close friends.

I kissed her hand, happily inhaling the familiar scent of her lotion. "We will make it work. You are going to adore Florence."

"I know. I'm excited. I'm really glad you convinced me to apply." She glanced down, suddenly looking nervous. "And this may be totally inappropriate to say, and I don't expect you to say it back or anything, but I thought you should know, I love you."

I grinned. She was adorable when she blushed. I was tempted to make her squirm longer, but I couldn't help it. Not telling her how I felt thus far had nearly killed me. "Ti voglio bene," I said, which roughly translated to 'I love you a lot.'

Bridget bit her bottom lip. "You always have to one up me, huh."

We spent the next few hours slowly exploring the town, hand in hand, before boarding our train. Bridget was clearly exhausted, but even though I encouraged her to nap, she was too eager to catch her first glimpse of the Italian countryside to sleep much. Finally, about an hour from our destination, she dozed off. She was facing the window still, but half curled against my lap. Logically, I knew I should try to rest too, since we wouldn't get to sleep until late tonight and would both have an early morning. Instead, I just watched her sleep.

She was so, so beautiful. I recognized my own bias, but that wasn't it. Everyone seemed to notice her. It was especially obvious in Europe, where the gawking men made little attempt to mask their joy at having such a gorgeous specimen cross their path. It was hard to believe that a woman this perfect could actually love me, but hearing from her first that this wasn't just a physical connection for her was the most wonderful thing ever.

For weeks, I had wanted to tell her how I felt. I told

myself my hesitation was because of our professional relationship. Somehow, telling my student I was in love with her seemed even more improper than sleeping with her several times each week. But honestly, I'd stalled because I hadn't known for certain how she would reply.

Now that I knew she felt the same way I did, I wasn't sure what that meant for us. Even in Italy, we couldn't parade our relationship, and when we returned to campus, we'd still have to tread lightly. There'd be a lot of red tape to cross surely. And for what? I wasn't so naïve as to believe there would actually be some happy ending for us at the end of the tunnel.

Bridget was twenty-one years old, focused on parties and friendships and likely grad school. She wasn't ready to settle down. She shouldn't be ready for marriage or kids, but my mind already flitted there. I couldn't help but think how adorable our kids would look or what a fun mom she'd be, but what I should be focused on is helping her pick a grad school program and have a fun senior year.

That night, when we'd settled into bed in my apartment, we talked for a while. I asked if she was nervous about starting classes and she replied casually in the negative. I laughed. Only Bridget could start college level courses in a foreign country without the slightest hint of anxiety.

"Are you?" she asked.

"Yeah," I said.

She traced a finger along my bare chest. "Well, having experienced your classes, I can say truthfully that you are a phenomenal teacher, so I'm pretty sure you'll do great. But even if you fail miserably, you still get to spend the summer in this gorgeous country with this gorgeous girl wrapped around your sexy body, so it's really a win-win either way."

I laughed, constantly surprised by her optimism. I was tempted to point out that my failing here could have serious ramifications for my future career prospects and that her failing could jeopardize her scholarship, but why drag her down with my realistic view? Besides, she was already slipping off her shirt, ready to distract me from my worries.

We made love slowly that night, as we both knew it might be our last chance to be together in that way for a while. When I thought she was close to climaxing, she paused, gripping my legs with her hips, and stared straight into my eyes.

"Tell me again," she said.

It took me a moment to realize what she wanted, but once the words "ti amo" left my mouth, she shattered into pieces, her body spasming around me tightly until I too found my release.

BRIDGET

Italy was a dream. I mean, obviously. How could it not be? After exploring France with my sexy travel companion, I'd been concerned Italy wouldn't meet my high expectations, but it truly surpassed them.

My dorm room on campus was larger than the ones back home, but oddly configured. My roommate was a quiet but nice girl from Milwaukee. We each had our own loft bed with a desk beneath. There was a small window overlooking the most charming street ever, and then a lot of open space. We each had a dresser, but the room altogether lacked any sort of closet. The bathroom was a common one, at the end of the hall, so I was stuck storing all my toiletries in our room as well. I rigged up a system to hang some of my clothes from the bed and managed to roll most of my skirts and tops that had to go in the dresser so as to avoid massive wrinkling, but I also ended up storing quite a few things at Owen's place.

His small studio apartment was about ten minutes away

by foot. He drew the path for me on a map, but instructed me never to walk the route alone at night or early in the morning. I saw zero signs that his safety concerns were warranted or that Florence was anything but the idyllic utopia I'd imagined, but I agreed to indulge his endearing paranoia. His apartment was minuscule but cozy. There was a kitchenette when you first entered—a mini fridge, two burner stove, sink, small counter top, and toaster/microwave combo thing. Three barstools against the end of the countertop formed the dining area, and just past that was a couch, chair, and coffee table. A small television was perched on top of a dresser between the chair and the bed, and a fireplace was on the other side of the bed. He had a small closet along the back wall and on the other side of the wall was the tiniest bathroom I'd ever seen.

In America, I supposed you would only find such a small place in the projects, but here, it was just charming. When I left after the first night there, I found myself daydreaming about sharing a similar apartment with Owen someday. Growing up, I'd always assumed I'd live in a large suburban house much like the one I'd occupied as a child. But now, I could actually see the romance in such a small home.

I had no solid guesses as to Owen's salary, but I figured it was paltry. I'd never fantasized about being broke as an adult, but I'd also never really wanted what my parents had. They loved each other, I supposed, and it wasn't a bad marriage by any means, but they were always so stressed out. Listening to them argue over who was supposed to call the lawn company or reschedule the cleaners made me wonder if true love even existed.

I couldn't imagine ever caring about such mundane, trivial matters with Owen. Together, we'd live a simpler life and it maybe wouldn't involve a large, fancy house, but that didn't matter. I never wanted to be more than a few feet away from him anyway.

When I had told him I loved him, I felt silly at first. I half expected him to laugh and chastise me, like the immature student that I was, falling head over heels for my teacher. But of course he hadn't. He had flashed that super sexy heart-melting smile of his and told me he felt the exact same way about me. He'd looked relieved, like he'd been waiting to tell me for weeks. And when he repeated it later that night, it validated every fantasy I'd ever had about our future.

I was positive this summer was going to be fantastic. I got to spend the next two months in the most romantic place on earth with the man I loved. After I flew home, I was scheduled to take a beach vacation with Stella, and then, when we returned to school, Owen and I would no longer have to hide from the world. Everything was perfect.

The first week of classes was rough. Being an immersion program, the classes were entirely in Italian. I was pleased to see that a fair chunk of the assigned homework required us to get out and explore the city rather than hole up in our dorm rooms completing worksheets. There were also several class field trips scheduled. Mondays and Thursdays our classes met on campus while Tuesdays and Wednesdays were reserved for field trips. My Italian art history class would be visiting eight different local museums over the summer, including of course the Uffizi gallery and the Galleria dell'Accademia. My class on the Medici family, which combined a fair amount of actual historical lessons with some Italian-language fiction about the Medicis, was set to tour the Boboli Gardens and several other historic palaces once inhabited by the famed family. My Tuscan culture class covered pretty much every other key tourist attraction in the area.

Owen was teaching a class on architecture to the American students in the program as well as a class on English grammar to the Italian students in the program. Because we lacked any significant overlap in our daytime schedules, we didn't see each other as often as I'd anticipated. The university promoted a few group field trips in the late afternoon on lecture days, so I got to climb to the top of Il Duomo with Owen…and a dozen of my other classmates and professors, and participate in a full lineup of festivities on St. John the Baptist day.

My plan had been to travel to other parts of Italy over the weekends, but Owen insisted I pass the first weekend in Florence, rounding out my view of the local attractions. The first weekend, we spent Saturday in the San Lorenzo district, eating our way through Mercato Centrale, then crossed the river into the Oltrarno district to see the city skyline at sunset from Piazzale Michelangelo. It had been the most romantic day I could imagine, topping even our first weekend in Paris.

OWEN

My concerns about Bridget being clingy in Florence were completely unwarranted. By the end of her first week on campus, she'd somehow befriended a handful of her classmates, organized a dinner party for the students at a local restaurant, and snagged an invite to a private traveling show in an art gallery near campus. None of this should have been surprising. Bridget's outgoing personality guaranteed her instant connections wherever she went, and her enthusiasm was contagious.

There were no classes on Fridays, so she invited me to a yoga class, an invitation that I politely declined. But when I texted her hours later, still seeing no sign of her on campus, she replied that she was still at Spiaggia Sull'Arno. I hadn't realized the urban beach, if it could be called that despite its location along the river and not a true sea, even offered yoga, but apparently it was a popular activity with the locals.

I took the bus to meet her after lunch. Just as I was about to text again, seeking clarification on her precise location, I noticed a group of young Italian men in the center of the beach. As I stepped closer, I spotted Bridget and a couple other girls from campus right in the center of everything. Of course. I laughed aloud, then I watched for a moment, amused that she had attracted the attention of enough local men to form a full Italian football team.

The girls had spread out towels and were all clad in bikinis, but Bridget, as always, was the breathtaking one. She wore a simple white string bikini, but the pale suit contrasted dramatically with her tanned skin and bold red hair. As I watched, she accepted a drink from one of the men closest to her, sipped, then handed it back. I tensed immediately. Due to the imported sand, I had to remove my sandals to even walk quickly towards her, and thankfully, once I was close, she stood and waved happily, causing her entourage to part enough to let me through.

"Owen!" she shrieked, quickly correcting herself to say, "Professore Chambers."

I had to laugh at the ridiculousness of the scene. Clearly, she was intoxicated, at 3PM on a weekday, in a foreign country, wearing nothing but a scrap of clothing. But she was so happy that it was hard to be upset with her.

"Who are all your friends?" I asked.

She gestured to the men closest to her. "This is Antonio, Giovanni, and Stefano."

She turned as the third man said something to her and then she repeated his name a few more times, clearly struggling with the pronunciation, or at least which syllable received the emphasis.

She gestured to the one holding the glass I'd seen her drink from. "Piero here works at a vineyard nearby. He said I am welcome to visit anytime."

"I'm sure he did," I said, reaching for her arm. "Can we talk for a moment?"

She nodded, then turned to her followers. "Scusatemi signori."

We had to walk thirty yards up the beach to be far enough from the DJ to speak in normal voices.

"I'm glad you came," she said, smiling.

"Are you? You seemed to be having a pretty good time without me," I said, instantly regretting the tenor of my words.

"Italians are just so friendly," she said, either missing my implication altogether or just ignoring it.

"Bridg, you're half naked and look like a goddess. Men of any nationality would be friendly."

She glanced down at her suit then back up to me. "It's a beach. You should be thankful I haven't taken off my top."

Now I laughed. "Sweetie, this isn't even a nude beach."

"I don't think anyone would complain."

"No, I don't imagine they would." I sighed. "But the same basic rules apply here as back home. You wouldn't accept a drink from a strange guy in the U.S., would you?"

She crossed her arms in front of her chest. "If it was fresh wine from his family vineyard, I would."

I sighed, feeling decades older at the realization that she spoke the truth. "Bridget…"

She rolled her eyes. "It was just a few sips, and I'm not alone. Katelyn and Amanda are here. And now you are, too."

"You seem a little tipsy for only a few sips."

"Oh, well, yeah. We started the day with brunch and there was super yummy sparkling prosecco."

"You drank wine before yoga?"

"Sparkling wine, and it was mixed with orange juice," she clarified. "Now stop being such a wet blanket and come have fun." She tried to drag me back towards her towel setup.

I glanced over at her classmates. Amanda was in one of my classes, but Katelyn was not. I didn't want to come off as the creepy teacher spending the day with my bikini-clad students, but I did really want to stay with Bridget, and only in part because it seemed she needed a babysitter.

She turned back to me. "Owen, it doesn't matter if they start to suspect there's something going on between us. They won't be able to prove anything and who cares what they think? We won't see them again after the end of this summer." She paused. "Besides, I may have already told them I had the hots for you and invited you along. So you won't have to worry about them hitting on you."

I relented and let her drag me back to the blanket. I half expected the Italian men to depart when they realized the girls now had a chaperone, but they didn't. As I started chatting with them, I decided Bridget hadn't been such a terrible judge of character after all. The men were all very nice, and Piero's wine was pretty tasty. But if Bridget was visiting that winery, it would be on my arm and not his.

CHAPTER 16

OWEN

*L*eaving Italy was hard. Returning to the states was never easy after spending any measure of time in Europe, with the long flight home being infinitely more miserable than the fight out had been, but this was particularly rough. I flew alone, and had the entire stretch of time to think about what the future held. I wasn't delusional enough to imagine long term plans with Bridget, but after the summer we'd shared, I couldn't help but look forward to the next semester.

We planned to maintain our secret for the first few weeks of the semester so as to avoid suspicion, but by fall break, we'd stop hiding. I didn't anticipate immediate support from everyone, but as I was no longer her professor, there was no firm reason we couldn't be together. Just thinking about all the places I wanted to take her once we could be in public as a couple was exhilarating.

I had over a week to spare before I needed to return to

campus, so I spent a few days with my family, and then drove out to see my friend Scott. Living in different towns, we didn't hang out as often as we'd like, but each time we met up, we picked up right where we'd left off.

We met up at a crowded chain for drinks and dinner, and I gave Scott an overview of my summer travels while we perused the menu.

"So what's new with you?" I asked as soon as the waitress left with our menus.

Scott sipped his beer and set it back on the waxed wood table before catching me up on his love life, new car, and career. Our meals arrived by the time he finished and asked me about life as a professor. I gave him the overview, then told him a few amusing stories from the classroom.

"So are you still a different woman every night kind of guy?" he asked with a mischievous smirk as we ordered another round of beers.

I laughed. "When was I ever that type of guy?"

"You were pretty busy senior year of high school. And you weren't doing so bad in college until you settled down with that one chick."

"Laura," I said.

"But she's out of the picture still, right?"

I chewed a bite of my burger. "We broke up nearly two years ago."

"In other words, you've had six hundred days of different women? Start talking."

We both laughed.

"Seriously, look at you, dude. If I were a single chick, I'd do you," Scott said, making us both laugh harder.

"And that is why you're my best friend," I teased. It felt good to hang out with Scott again. Conversation flowed quickly and freely with him and we were both always laughing.

We moved onto a different topic until we finished our food, but then somehow the discussion circled back to my dating life.

"I hate to disappoint but it definitely hasn't been that kind of a year, dating-wise. Nowhere close to 365 women."

"300?"

I shook my head.

"200? Come on, 50?"

I raised my hands up as though I didn't know what I'd done wrong to manage not to sleep with fifty women in a year.

"5?"

I sighed, then motioned for the waitress to bring us one last round. I could tell where this was headed.

"I went out with one chick a couple times after Laura and I broke up, but she was a flake," I finally said. "And then I took this woman from an art gallery out once, but that was a disaster. I didn't even sleep with her."

Scott frowned. "Tell me you haven't been chaste a full year."

I hesitated and glanced around us furtively. We were in the corner booth, and no other customers were nearby. Even if they were, the chances of them hearing our conversation over the TVs blaring various sports throughout the restaurant were slim.

"There's been one woman," I said, leaning forward.

"I knew it!" He pounded his fist proudly against the table. "Spill."

"Here's the thing. We can't exactly broadcast the relationship, so…"

"What?"

"It's totally under wraps. Literally no one knows that I'm involved with this woman except me and her, and Olivia. She keeps my number under a fake name on her phone."

Scott was clearly fascinated by this entire discussion. "Forbidden fruit, eh?"

I laughed, nodding.

"So she's married?"

"No."

He proceeded to list the various scenarios he figured would necessitate secrecy, with me shaking my head after each. "In the mafia? In prison? A distant cousin? A not-so-distant cousin? Your sister's best friend? Your mother's best friend? Some other really old lady?"

We were both laughing by the time he said "Underage?"

I hesitated a moment too long on that one.

"Seriously, that's it? She's underage?" Scott looked surprised, but I guess as my friend he felt compelled to withhold the look of disgust.

"No, she's younger, but she's not underage. She's almost 22."

He shrugged. "That's not that big of an age diff..." his voice trailed off. "Oh. I see."

I waited to see if he'd really figured it out, but he quickly mouthed the word "student," so I was sure.

"So, there's the dilemma," I said.

He took a few swigs of his beer while contemplating my situation. "Here's the thing, Owen. You have always been popular with the ladies. You probably didn't notice, but even our waitress was flirting with you tonight."

I had suspected as much, but didn't see the relevance. "What's your point?"

"I don't know. Couldn't you like, lose your job, for dating her?"

I drank a long gulp from my beer before nodding.

Scott shook his head. "She must be really hot."

I pulled out my phone and clicked on the first photo of her I found. She was wearing ridiculously short denim shorts and a long, flowing white tank top, posing happily by the Coliseum. Her hair, now back to strawberry blonde, fell gracefully over one shoulder. The picture could be mistaken as one from a professional photo shoot since she looked so impeccable, but, of course, it was just a casual pose for Bridget.

Scott's eyes widened. "Yeah, okay, so she is definitely really hot. And I'm sure the sex is phenomenal."

I nodded. He rolled his eyes resentfully.

"But that doesn't mean it's worth it. You have to think with your brain, not with your…" He halted his sentence as the waitress reappeared to refill our waters and clear away our mostly empty plates.

Scott continued. "What happens when she gets tired of you? Or when she gets a bad grade on a test? Or asks for a better grade? Or when you want to break up with her?"

"Honestly? Nothing. She's a good student. And she's not vengeful or anything."

"No woman is vengeful until you break her heart, and then she'll be crying rape to the dean."

"Not Bridget. In fact, we sort of broke up for a week before spring break, and nothing like that happened. She didn't tell anyone, she didn't do anything to jeopardize my career."

"Spring break," he repeated. "So how long have you been seeing her?"

"About eight months."

I wouldn't have thought it possible, but his eyes opened even wider.

"Owen you've been talking about being a college professor since we were like ten. It's not worth it."

I drained the rest of my beer. "I think maybe she is."

. . .

Bridget

I spent one week at home post-Italy before heading down south with Stella for a much-needed beach vacay. I hadn't realized how much I'd missed Stella all summer, nor how hard it would be to tell her all about my trip without letting on any details about Owen. Luckily, she'd had a busy summer too, having dumped Jerrod and then hooked up with a guy at her family's country club. So, Stella had her fair share of stories to tell, too.

We spent the first two days at the beach, lounging in the sun, drinking and playing music, but the third day looked overcast. So we drove to the nearest mall to shop. The sun had just begun to peak out from behind the clouds when we cruised back to our condo.

I was driving quickly so we could hit up the beach, but we were both rocking out to the music. Stella was belting out song after song like we were in a karaoke bar, which was hilarious.

Stella fell quiet as the music abruptly stopped and an obnoxious voice informed us of an incoming call. I glanced away from the road briefly to check the caller ID. It was Owen, but of course Enzo was the name that flashed on the screen. I tapped the breaks, quickly fumbling for the button to send the call into voice mail. I knew there was a way to answer the call with my actual phone rather than through the speaker system of the car, but I didn't trust myself to press the right button and certainly didn't want to risk broadcasting the call so Stella could hear.

"Answer?" she asked, finger poised over a button. I had forgotten that she was much more technologically savvy than me. Not that it was any big feat to be better than me at it.

"Voice mail please," I said, exhaling with relief and returning my eyes to the road.

She pressed a button and there was a pause and a click, then just when I expected the music to resume, I heard Owen's voice instead.

"Ciao Bella," he said.

I felt my eyes widen and I turned to Stella.

"Sorry, I think I made it play the voice mail out loud. This is all different from on my car."

I reached for the volume and tried to mute it, but the radio controls had no effect on the message. His voice continued to ring loudly through the car.

"I had some good news for you, tesoro mio, so call me when you have a chance. Also, I have a pensierino per te. Nothing much, so don't get excited. But call me. Sei il sole della mia vita."

There was another click and the music resumed. I hadn't realized I'd been holding my breath until I exhaled with a loud swoosh. My face felt uncomfortably warm, and I could tell Stella was staring at me, but I was scared to make eye contact with her. How would I explain why my professor was calling me his treasure? Or the sun in his life? There was no plausible explanation for that.

"Who was that?" Stella asked.

"Oh, um, Professor Chambers."

"Does he always do that?" Stella asked calmly.

I turned to her. She looked confused, but not shocked.

"Umm, do what?"

"Speak half in Italian and half in English. That was Italian, right?"

I considered her words and smiled. I hadn't fully processed the fact that Owen's message was almost entirely in a language Stella didn't speak.

"Yes. I mean, he's the professor, so it's kind of his job, I guess."

Stella glanced down at her phone. Relief washed over me

as she began typing away, clearly unaffected by my odd voice mail.

"I've never had a professor call me."

"We got to know each other pretty well during the study abroad thing. He said he was calling me about the degree program anyway."

She nodded, then glanced up from her phone. "Tesoro. That means treasure?"

My breath caught in my throat and I struggled to recall a similar word. "Oh, uh, yeah, but he said tuo zelo, which means your zeal. Um, you know, like my study ethic."

I turned briefly to find Stella staring at me skeptically.

"It's a long story," I continued. "Sort of an inside joke."

I caught Stella nodding out of the corner of my eye.

"Sure, an inside joke with a professor. Makes sense to me. Well, you can call him back if you want. You must be anxious to hear what he had to say about your degree thing."

"I'm sure it's nothing urgent."

Stella was quiet for a few minutes, but just when I finally started to relax and assume I was out of the woods, she spoke again. "So you told me about your classes and everything but what about the rest? Any hot Italian men sweep you off your feet?"

I laughed. "No, sadly no Italian men waiting to seduce me."

"Who all did you travel around with at the end? Anyone from campus here?"

"Uh, it was a group of students from a bunch of different universities. No one you know."

"When do I get to see pictures?"

"I thought I showed you them."

"You showed me some." She reached towards my phone. "Are they on your photo roll? I can scroll through now."

"No!" I shouted just as she grabbed my phone.

Stella placed my phone to her right and calmly watched me as I struggled to reach over her without veering the car off the road.

"Stella, I swear if you don't give me my phone back right now..." I began. I stopped myself, because I didn't really have any legit threats I could carry out while driving. Also, I realized she wasn't even trying to look at my phone anymore. Instead she was just eying me.

"I thought we were best friends. What exactly don't you want me to see? Lots of nude selfies?"

"We are, and it's nothing. I'll just show you the pictures later."

"I thought your Professor's name was Owen. The hot one. Wasn't that the one who came with you to Italy, Owen Chambers?"

I forced a chuckle. "He didn't exactly come with me, but yes, that's the professor the university sent."

"Why does his name show up as Enzo on caller ID?"

I didn't answer. I had no way to explain everything and Stella clearly wasn't buying it anyway.

"Bridge?"

I sighed. "It's a joke. One of his first professors couldn't remember his name and called him Enzo instead of Owen."

Stella handed my phone back and turned to her window. She was quiet again, but I knew the discussion wasn't over. Finally, she looked at me again. "Look, I get why you can't say anything at school, but it's just us in the car now, and if there's something you want to tell me, I hope you know you can trust me. I'm fairly certain I have a good idea of what's going on anyway, and it hurts my feelings that you won't just tell me."

I blew out a breath. I had been naïve to think I could hide Owen from Stella. She knew me too well. "It's not just my secret to tell. And if people found out, there could be real consequences."

"I'm not people, I'm me."

I took a long swig from my water bottle, weighing my words carefully. "Stella, what do you want me to say?"

"I don't know, maybe that your much older professor is trying to seduce you and you don't really know what to do?"

I choked on my water. "That's what you think is going on?" I turned to my friend.

She frowned, then nodded.

"First off, he's not that old. He's still in his twenties, you know? And second of all, no one is seducing anyone."

"What exactly happened in Italy with you guys?"

"It was a good trip. I completed the intensive course and traveled around some, just like I told you." I paused. "Owen and I are friends. Good friends. And I didn't want to travel around on my own, so he came with me. Not as some creepy older guy trying to seduce me, but as my friend."

I was aware that Stella was still eying me warily, probably trying to decipher if I was lying. I felt I'd been convincing enough. Everything I said was the truth, really. Owen and I were friends. And soon, we could stop hiding the rest.

* * *

THE NEXT DAY, Stella and I were back on the beach, trying to get a picture of the both of us with the ocean in the background.

"Here, my arms are longer," she said, snatching my phone away. She clicked a few and then pulled the phone closer to check her work while I refilled our drinks.

I wiped my damp hands off on the towel and returned to my seat. Stella was eying me suspiciously.

"What?"

She held my phone out. "You got a text."

Between the daiquiris and the days of relaxation with my best friend, I was feeling too calm to interpret her expression with an adequate level of panic. I took my phone back and slowly clicked over to my messages, still watching my friend out of the corner of my eye. When I saw the message was from "Enzo," a lump formed in the pit of my stomach.

"The campus is nothing w/out you bellissima. Hurry back. Ti amo *tanto*."

I read the message twice before deciding if there was any way to dismiss it as a friend text. Then I turned to Stella, ready to explain it off.

She took one look at me, shook her head, and settled back against her chair. "Don't even bother. I may not be a budding linguist like you but I'm pretty sure I can guess the translation of 'ti amo,' and it isn't 'hey buddy.'"

I felt tears brimming in my eyes. "He's been my professor, Stella. I couldn't say anything."

She sat abruptly. "Who did you think I was going to tell?"

I didn't answer immediately. I truly did trust her to keep my secret, but it felt like I was betraying Owen. "I didn't think you would tell anyone if I asked you not to, but Owen and I agreed to keep it a secret. Now that he isn't my professor anymore, I was going to tell you soon anyway."

"Really?" Her tone filled with disbelief.

"Yes! We just wanted to wait until classes started so no one questioned when the relationship started. It's been so hard keeping this from you, Stella."

Her expression softened. "You lied right to my face when I asked you about it after he called. You said you were good friends."

"We are."

She snorted. "So you aren't sleeping with him?"

I sighed.

"And when did that start? This summer?"

I swallowed.

"Jesus. Sooner?"

"You know we got to know each other outside of class. He was in my Creole class and we became friends then. It just… progressed, from there."

"So you were sleeping with him while he was your professor?"

"It's not just sex," I said.

"Oh my God," she mumbled. "No wonder your grades are so good. Thank goodness you didn't break up with him before finals."

"Stella! Seriously? Maybe I was right to not tell you. I can't believe you're even judging me about that. You know I earned all of my grades."

She sighed, taking a moment to calm down. "I know, I know. It just, well, it's creepy and cliché. He should know better."

"Look, I can see why it might sound shady to you, but Owen never pressured me into anything. He's never been anything but mature and patient and supportive. And he is risking his entire career just to be with me so I'm not really inclined to listen to you insult him."

Stella shot me a look that showed no signs of remorse, then settled back into her chair.

I packed up my stuff as quickly as I could, glared at her one last time, then trudged back up the beach and into the hotel. I rinsed the sand off in the shower, then quickly dressed and plopped onto my stomach at the foot of the bed.

I dialed Owen, and he answered on the first ring. "Hey, I was just thinking about you. How's the beach?"

"Good," I said, biting back tears. "Do you have a minute?"

"Sure. What's wrong?"

I hesitated. "Stella saw the text you just sent me."

There was a lengthy silence, followed by, "oh."

"When you called yesterday and left me that voice mail about the scholarship, Stella heard that, and I was able to play that off since you apparently speak a decent mixture of Italian and English. But then she saw the text and..." I sniffled.

"So she knows," he concluded calmly.

"Yes. I mean, I didn't tell her everything, but she definitely has the gist."

"And the timeline?"

"Yeah."

There was an extended pause.

"Don't worry cuore mio. It's fine. We were going to tell people soon anyway."

I tried to stifle my tears. It was hard to be too sad when he referred to me as "my heart." Of course, if he didn't have to be so over the top with the damn romance all the time, Stella may not have figured it out.

"Bridget, come on. Why are you sad? This is not a big deal. You know I told my sister and Scott."

I did know that, but it wasn't reassuring. Owen and his sister were super close, so I never would've asked him to keep our relationship from her. And even though it should be the same for him to tell his best friend as for me to tell mine, it didn't feel that way. If we were caught, Owen was the one with a lot to lose, not me. I didn't want to risk doing or saying anything that would jeopardize his dream of teaching.

"Stella's mad that I didn't tell her sooner, and she doesn't get it. She thinks you're some creepy older guy using your magical gradebook power to seduce me."

The low vibrating hum of Owen's soft laughter relaxed me. "A lot of people would think that if they knew," he said.

"She's my best friend, Owen. She should know I wouldn't sleep with someone to up my grade."

"Oh babe, she does know. She's just upset that you kept something this big from her. She'll come around."

We talked for another fifteen or twenty minutes, and then Stella came in.

"I should go. Stella is back now."

"Okay. Ti amo."

"Me too," I said, hanging up. I turned to Stella slowly.

"The professor?"

I nodded.

She slowly approached me. "Look, I'm sorry, okay. I guess I could have reacted better. I just worry about you."

"I know. And I'm sorry for not telling you. Maybe part of me was nervous about how you'd react."

Stella laughed. "So you really love him?"

I nodded.

"Was he upset that I found out?"

"No."

She sighed, climbing onto the bed and making herself comfortable. "Okay. Tell me all the juicy details."

I leaned in to hug her, glad she was so understanding.

CHAPTER 17

OWEN

The first week of classes went off without a hitch, but then, that Saturday, I got an urgent call from Professor Lazarro. I wasn't sure what to expect when the department head called me into his office, on a weekend no less. My first instinct was to panic. Someone must have seen Bridget and I together, or maybe Stella tattled on us.

I tried to reassure myself that maybe it was a good thing or even standard practice, for the department head to call a new professor into the office on a Saturday. My efforts failed, though, and by the time I shook Professor Lazarro's hand on my way into his office, my palms were damp with sweat.

Professor Lazarro made small talk for a few minutes before launching into the issue.

"I'm sorry to drag you in here on a Saturday, but I've just learned that Professor Rizzo has to take the rest of the semester off for health reasons."

"Oh no. I hope he's okay," I said, guilt-ridden over the fact that I felt relief at hearing I was here because my colleague was sick and not because I was sleeping with my former student.

"Well, he assures me he will be, but he's going to need surgery and isn't sure how long the recovery will be, so we agreed it would be best to plan on him missing the entire semester. But that means I need to divvy up his classes, and fast."

"I understand. I'm happy to help," I said, already worried about the stress an additional class would place on my schedule. The extra money would be nice, but maybe not enough to compensate for the pressure.

"I already asked Professor Mancini to take over Professor Rizzo's 200 level class, and his other 300 level courses may be a bit intense for you so early in the department, but I think you'd be a perfect fit for his Intensive Grammar course. It's a larger class since it's required for all majors, but he's already prepared the syllabus and the textbook is pretty straightforward."

"Sure, sure," I said, trying to convince myself as much as Professor Lazarro that I could handle it. Despite my fluency in the language, I really hadn't taught many upper level courses yet. So it could get a bit hairy if I had one of the harder classes.

Professor Lazarro thanked me and shook my hand. Then, he politely hurried me out so he could meet with the next replacement professor. It wasn't until I was back at my own office that I realized Bridget was taking Intensive Grammar this semester. I quickly logged into the course catalog, praying there were multiple sections, but there was only one.

I locked my office and returned to Professor Lazarro's office, catching him right as he was heading out.

"Sorry to disturb you," I began, "But I was thinking it

would be better for me to take over the 200 level course and for Professor Mancini to handle the Grammar course. I already have a 200 level course and he's so experienced at Grammar."

My boss frowned at me. "It's all set up already. Besides, I think the 200 level course conflicts with your 150 class. This is really the only arrangement that works. I really need you to handle this one."

I swallowed the lump in my throat. What was I supposed to say—that I couldn't because I wanted to date one of the students? I certainly couldn't admit the relationship had already begun.

With no options, I assured him I could handle it, thanked him again, and trekked back to my office.

BRIDGET

Owen was a mess when I arrived at his apartment that night. I hadn't even taken off my shoes when he spilled the entire story. And I was in such a good mood since my Italian grammar class had been cancelled that morning that I didn't even realize the ramifications of what he was saying right away.

"So you're going to be my professor again?" I finally put together.

He nodded.

I shrugged. "Well, so nothing changes then, right?"

Owen winced. "You could drop the class. Take it next semester."

"I can't. It's a prerequisite to the two classes I have to take next semester."

"Shit," he mumbled, flopping backwards onto his pillow.

I stretched out beside him, placing my head on his chest. He'd showered and changed into his sexy undershirt since I'd seen him that morning. The material was soft under my cheek, a nice contrast to his hard abs beneath my hand.

"It's not so bad," I said. "Last semester was fine, right? We just can't tell anyone yet. No big deal."

"Bridget, that means we still have to hide. I can't take you out to movies or dinners or concerts or anything. Basically we have another three months where we can only be together in here like this."

I inhaled his masculine smelling cologne and smiled. "I'm okay with that. I could stay here forever."

He kissed my head. "Ti amo, but you deserve to go out and have fun."

"I do go out and have fun. It would be nice to be able to do things in public together, but be serious, Owen. It's not like you would've taken me to my sorority's formal dance or hit up the Sigma Chi party with me."

"I just hate feeling like we're hiding."

"I think it's a turn on."

"Are you using me for sex?" Owen teased.

I smiled, loving the way that sounded. "Now you're just trying to tempt me."

He forced a smile, but his pout returned within a moment. I hated seeing him so stressed. I stood and reached for his hand.

"Dance with me," I commanded.

"There's no music."

I grabbed my phone, scrolled through the playlist, then tugged his hand harder as the song started. "Dance with me," I said again, this time my voice a mere whisper.

Owen cracked a smile. "You have Righteous Brothers on your phone? Will you ever stop surprising me?"

"I hope not," I said, sighing happily as he pressed his body against mine and began to sway to the soulful melody.

When the song ended, Owen kissed my neck, still holding

me close. And I knew without a doubt that he was infinitely more relaxed now.

* * *

THE NEXT FEW weeks were fine. I was more acutely aware of the downside our secret romance than I had been before, and every day, I grew more eager to tell the world Owen Chambers was all mine. But I had no major complaints. My classes were all French and Italian, which was oddly refreshing. And being a senior had definite perks, especially at the sorority. Stella and I now had our own bedroom that we could actually sleep in rather than the cold dorm, except it was rare for either of us to be there more than a couple nights a week.

Stella still wasn't exactly supportive of my relationship with Owen, but she wasn't so judgmental anymore either. And it was definitely a relief to be able to talk with my best friend about him.

One night, I was at Owen's, talking on the phone with Stella, when he finally finished whatever he was grading. He glanced at me, grinned mischievously, then tugged his shirt off over his head. I adjusted my position on the couch so I could fully appreciate the view as he lifted weights. I suspected Owen wasn't really intending a full work out, but was rather just trying to tempt me off the phone faster. And it totally would've worked except Stella was in the middle of her spiel trying to convince me to go on the senior camping trip over fall break.

"You're not listening, Stella," I said, wiggling my eyebrows enthusiastically at Owen. "I don't camp. I don't even know what glamping is, but unless it involves air conditioning and an actual mattress not filled with air, I am not interested."

She tried to liken the experience to my Italy trip, and I cut her off.

"Not even remotely like Italy. I wasn't on a tour of sub-Saharan Africa, I was in the Mediterranean. Babe, I'm sorry, but you are going to have to tackle this adventure alone."

She accepted defeat and hung up.

Owen was still doing bicep curls.

"I feel like you'd get a better workout without your pants," I said.

He stepped closer to allow me to unfasten them for him.

"Was that Stella?" he asked.

I nodded. "She wants me to go camping over fall break. I could not be less interested."

"So what are your plans for fall break?"

I shrugged. "I guess I'll just go home, but since I'll be home again over Thanksgiving, I'm not thrilled about the prospect."

Owen tilted his head. "What if you came to my home instead?"

"You want me to stay here the whole break?" It actually wasn't a terrible idea, but it seemed like we might get bored being forced to hide away together without any distractions like class. I reached around him to start pulling his pants down.

He grinned. "Not this home, my old home, where my parents live."

I must have looked terrified, because he quickly added, "We'd stay at my sister's house, though."

I considered this for a moment, my hands still frozen on his ass. He set the weights on the carpet and hoisted himself over me, really blurring my ability to think clearly about the options.

"You want me to come with you?"

"I do," he said. "I figured you had plans or I would've brought it up sooner. You can meet my family, but also we'll be in a different town so we could maybe even venture out into public together."

I couldn't say no to that, and as he lowered his body slowly onto mine, there really wasn't anything I'd say no to.

CHAPTER 18

OWEN

*B*ridget's fidgeting told me she was nervous as we made our way to my hometown, but that didn't stop her from rocking out to Def Leppard, Van Halen, and several other bands I'd figured she was way too young to be into. We pulled into my sister's driveway around 8, and Olivia rushed out to greet us. She pulled me in for her typical overly abrasive hug and then offered a gentler version to Bridget.

"Nice to meet you again," she said to Bridget before introducing her to my brother-in-law Dave.

It was a nice night, so we had dinner on their back deck and then sat outside with drinks until late. Bridget was friendly during dinner, but still fairly tense. When we left the table, I pulled her beside me on the cushioned bench, wrapping my arm around her. I immediately felt her relax with the contact, so I made a point to stay physically close to her the rest of the evening.

"So what's the plan for tomorrow?" Olivia casually asked.

I glanced at Bridget. "I thought I'd take her around town and show her some of our old haunts. We're meeting Scott for lunch, and then we'll head over to Mom and Dad's by 5."

"What did you tell them exactly?" she asked.

The question was vague, but I knew what she was asking. "I told them I was bringing the girl I've been seeing who I met in my Creole literature class. Mom asked if she was an Italian grad student last year like me and I said no, that she was studying French."

"Does Mom know there's an age difference with you guys?"

"No, but I can't see why that would be an issue. I mean, ideally we won't need to discuss that Bridget may have historically taken a class of mine, but..."

Olivia snorted. "Good luck with that." She stood and stretched. "I'd stay up later, but I have to work in the morning."

I stood and said good night.

She turned to Bridget, then me. "Honestly Owen, Mom is going to love her. Both of them will. And they'll probably be too distracted by how clearly out of your league she is to even question the rest."

Bridget turned to me once Olivia was inside. "Do you think she's right?"

I nodded. My parents are not intimidating people and besides, Bridget was very likeable. A person would have to really try to find some fault with her.

* * *

As PREDICTED, everyone loved Bridget. She and Scott hit it off great at lunch, so much so that he actually declared, "I totally get it man. She does seem worth it," via text after we got together.

My parents were similarly taken by Bridget from the moment they met her.

Bridget reiterated my story about how we'd met in the graduate level French course but didn't start dating till later. When my mom asked if she'd presented her thesis yet, she answered truthfully by saying no, but that she hoped to teach at the university level after grad school. My parents knew she was younger, but probably not how much younger, and the fact that they seemed to assume she was a grad student wasn't entirely our fault.

The best part of the entire trip was pretending to be a normal couple for a few days. We went to restaurants together, held hands as we walked around town together, and on Saturday night we went out to a local bar with Olivia and Dave.

The bar was slightly crowded and dimly lit. A local band was playing covers of hit songs and we couldn't hear each other without shouting. We were all carded on entering, an occurrence I had to attribute to Bridget's presence, since my sister and I had frequented that bar for years without our ID's being checked. I gazed around, seeing no sign of any people from campus. That wasn't surprising by any means, but I figured I'd confirm anyway before wrapping my arm around Bridget.

She stiffened at the contact, then turned to me.

"It's okay," I mouthed, and she smiled.

"Over here!" Dave shouted, gesturing wildly. We followed him and squeezed around the table he'd snagged. We ordered drinks and appetizers and attempted to talk, but mostly we could only hear each other in between the songs. Bridget was happily dancing in her seat, turning every few minutes to watch the band or enviously eye the people dancing by the stage.

I downed the rest of my beer then nudged Bridget. I knew Olivia would mock me till the end of time for this, but I couldn't let my girl sit out another song. Bridget squealed excitedly when she realized what I was doing and even though I pulled her out of her chair by her hand, she was the one to drag me all the way to the front by the stage. As soon as we reached the front, the song ended and a slower song played.

I relaxed, pulling Bridget closer.

She roped her arms around my neck, staring into my eyes for a minute, then rested her head against my chest. I kissed the top of her head, squeezed my hands into her hips and sighed. This, I had to admit, would be an excellent perk of being able to date publicly. The slow song ended, but by this point I was committed, so we kept dancing.

Bridget danced as though she didn't have a care in the world. She lacked any degree of self-consciousness, too, although if I looked like her while dancing, I probably wouldn't be self-conscious either. I felt some eyes on us, but assumed they were just checking out Bridget. I didn't dare to turn towards my sister, as she was surely laughing at me. We danced for a third song, but halfway through it, Bridget pulled me closer and swayed against me as though the song were designed for a slow dance. When the song ended, she winked and excused herself to the ladies' room.

I returned to the table alone, prepared to be mocked, but instead Olivia and Dave were smiling.

"You must really love her," Dave said.

"You guys are obnoxiously cute together," Olivia added.

I guessed those were both compliments. For me, seeing that we still functioned well when we weren't just holed up in my apartment making love was refreshing. Just maybe, there might actually be hope for us as a couple after this semester.

BRIDGET

After fall break, it was even harder not be with Owen all the time. The semester was halfway over, and I kept telling myself that my Christmas present would be the ability to stop hiding our relationship from the world, but it was a struggle to wait, nonetheless. And as much as I loved meeting Owen's family and friends, it made me a little jealous that he couldn't meet mine.

I didn't doubt that my parents would like him if they got to know him, but I was equally sure they would never even try to know him once they learned he was my teacher. Talking to my father was akin to what I imagined the Great Inquisition to be. It was less a conversation and more an interrogation where the examiner was really eager to find fault. Unfortunately, even if we stuck with our planned story and told my parents we started dating after I finished Owen's class, my dad would still hold against us the fact that he had previously been my teacher. So, I tried to just focus on the present.

My birthday came and went. I celebrated with Stella, enjoying brunch, massages, and shopping during the day. That evening, we continued the festivities with dinner, drinks, and dancing with the girls later. The next day was a Saturday, so I celebrated alone with Owen. He cooked a romantic dinner, gave me a gorgeous necklace he'd been hiding since leaving Italy, where he'd bought it, and he entertained me all night long. It was a good birthday.

On Thursday night, I was sleeping at Owen's again. Since I didn't have Friday classes, I always stayed at his place Thursdays. He still had to be on campus in the morning, but

I had my own key and just locked up for him if I left later than him.

Tonight, though, it was still dark when I felt Owen shift beside me. I slowly opened my eyes to find he had crept out of bed and seemed to be dressing.

"What are you doing?" I asked, yawning.

"Sorry, I just realized I left the papers I need tomorrow in my office. It's going to stress me out too much to sleep so I'm just going to go grab them and be back in a few minutes."

I sat up. "Okay, give me a minute to get dressed and you can drop me off on your way."

Owen knelt beside the bed and kissed my forehead. "It's two-thirty in the morning, Bridget. Go back to sleep. I'll lock up and be back in bed with you before you know it."

I was exhausted, so I agreed, drifting back to sleep before I even heard the click of the door shutting.

When I awoke a bit later, something was amiss. I heard a cacophony of noises from outside—voices, thumping, and vehicles. The room seemed darker than it should be and the air felt heavy. My entire body was fatigued, an exhaustion I'd previously only experienced during finals. I decided I was dreaming and stayed where I was.

A moment later, however, there was a loud thump, followed by a crash and a series of loud voices. Everything was still foggy though, and I was seeing and hearing everything as though under water. I heard my name called out, and a large figure loomed in the doorway.

I screamed, and the figure came closer.

"Fire department, Miss, stay calm," the man said.

Before I could protest, he had lifted me out of the bed, and a moment later, I was outside. As the cold air blasted into my eyes, I was instantly alert. Fire trucks surrounded the building, and a crowd of anxious, pajama-clad people stood watching the chaos. I couldn't see the building from my vantage point, and the thick suit of my rescuer blocked most of my view of the crowd.

"Owen," I said aloud, still confused.

Then I realized he might still be in the building. "Owen!" I shouted. "You have to go get Owen!"

"Hang on, Miss," the firefighter said, plopping me onto a stretcher beside an ambulance.

I immediately sat up, determined to make someone realize Owen was missing, but before I could scream again, he was there.

"Oh thank God, Bridget!" he said, grabbing my hand.

A female paramedic nudged him to the side, wrapped a mask over my face and tightened a cuff on my arm.

Owen's face was filled with panic. "Bridge, I'm so sorry. I wasn't gone that long, but I couldn't get close to the building when I came back because the firetrucks were here. They must have been called right after I left. I parked a block away and ran here and then as soon as I realized you weren't out I asked them to go get you. You could have been killed!"

"Sir," the paramedic said. "Step aside. You can speak with her in a moment."

Owen backed up, but kept a steady, nervous gaze on me. I closed my eyes for a moment, trying to take in everything that had happened, or rather, was ongoing. Finally, the paramedic tapped me and lifted my mask up.

"Miss, you seem fine, but we're going to take you in to the hospital just for observation. You may have breathed in some smoke or carbon monoxide."

I nodded weakly, unsure of whether or not I felt okay. Owen stepped closer, and still looked distraught.

"Bridget, when I came up and saw the fire..." his voice trailed off but he stepped closer and pressed his lips against the top of my head. "Ti amo tanto," he whispered.

"It's okay, I'm fine," I said. I tried to raise my head to see the building, to ascertain exactly what damage the fire caused and if it was under control yet, but I immediately noticed all eyes from the crowd were on us.

"Shit," I mumbled, realizing our mistake. "Owen back up. Everyone is watching us. They're going to figure out..." I didn't want to specify in case the paramedic was listening. "Just go away. I'm fine."

Owen paled, but didn't move. "Bridget, it's too late for that." He pressed his lips into my forehead again. "I'll meet you at the hospital," he said.

I nodded and was loaded into the ambulance. The next hour of my life was a blur—my first ambulance ride, my first ER visit, and the panic of the unknown status of my romantic and educational future.

It felt like an eternity before the nurse finally left my side and Owen was able to talk to me again.

I'm so sorry," he said, crouching beside the bed and squeezing my hand.

"Did you set the fire?"

He shook his head, confused. "I heard it was a candle in a third floor apartment."

"Then you don't need to apologize. None of this was your fault."

"Bridget, it was my fault you were in that apartment. I invited you over, I insisted you stayed when you offered to leave. I left you there, alone. No one else knew you were in that apartment, Bridget. When I got there, the firefighters thought everyone was out of the building. They told me everyone was out and it wasn't until I got closer and realized you weren't there that they sent someone back in. You could've died because of me."

He was on the verge of tears, and it pained me to watch.

"But I didn't, Owen. I'm fine." I paused. "The paramedic said the smoke rises, so it hadn't triggered the smoke detectors on the first floor yet. But I was so groggy when they came in that they were worried I breathed in some carbon monoxide."

He winced, and I regretted having told him that.

"I was calling your name like a crazy person," he admitted. "I was too scared to think straight. And then when they brought you out..." He sighed. "Everyone saw, Bridget. By tomorrow, everyone will know about us."

Dread settled over me like a heavy weight as he spoke. My stomach tightened uncomfortably, but I wasn't sure if it was from the smoke or the sense of doom I just couldn't shake.

"We'll figure something out, Owen," I said, not sounding the slightest bit convincing.

"There's nothing to figure out, Bridget. This isn't one of those situations where you can just bat your eyelashes and everyone will..."

"Mom!" I interrupted, my eyes wide with shock.

CHAPTER 19

BRIDGET

"$\mathcal{M}$om, I told you not to come," I said, as she looked me over with a frown.

She rolled her eyes and leaned in for a hug, apparently having concluded I was fine. "You called me from the hospital and said you were in a fire. Of course I was going to come."

"How did you get here so fast? It's at least a two hour drive."

"I left right when we spoke. How are you? The nurse said you would be discharged shortly?"

"I'm fine. Tired and a little shaken up, but fine." I glanced nervously at Owen, who was trying to appear invisible in the corner of the room.

My mom nodded and relaxed noticeably. Then she followed my gaze to Owen. "I'm sorry to have interrupted. I didn't know you had visitors." She turned to Owen and offered her hand. "I'm Barbara Williams."

"Owen Chambers," he said politely, shaking her hand. "Nice to meet you." Owen turned to me. "I should go."

I bit my lip and pleaded silently with him to stay. I didn't know where things stood with us, and it seemed likely that we might have to be apart for a while as soon as the news of the fire—and my location—got out.

"Don't leave on my account," my mother said.

He shook his head politely. "No, I need to get to class. Bridget, please call me if you need a ride home."

I mustered a weak smile, and he left.

My mother turned back to me the moment he was out of earshot. "I thought you didn't have a boyfriend."

"Owen is just a friend."

"Just a friend who visits you during a six hour observational hospital stay?"

I shrugged.

She inhaled sharply, looking concerned again. "Are you sure you're feeling okay? Tell me what happened exactly. It must have been terrifying."

I relayed the story of the fire to her in a disjointed fashion, as though I hadn't experienced it firsthand.

"So it was an apartment building that caught fire?"

I nodded.

"Whose apartment were you in at three o'clock in the morning?"

I took the opportunity to sip slowly out of my plastic hospital water cup in lieu of answering.

"Owen's?"

I didn't answer, and she interpreted my silence appropriately.

"What were you and your 'friend' doing in the middle of the night in his apartment?"

"I fell asleep studying. He wasn't there when the fire

started. He had gone to pick up some papers he left on campus."

She frowned. "This all sounds fishy."

I sighed, exasperated. "Look, mom, I'm fine, okay? Really! It was just really bad luck that I was in an apartment building when it caught fire, but it could've happened in my own building, so it's not worth dwelling on that little detail. Yes, I've been seeing Owen, but that's it. There's no more to the story. I'm twenty-two years old and I can date if I want."

My mother was silent for a moment, then grinned widely. "I knew you were dating someone," she said proudly. "He's cute," she said.

I blushed, desperate to think of a less awkward topic to discuss with my mom.

"What is his major?"

I hesitated, trying to select the most harmless lie. "Italian. He speaks French also, though."

"How old is he? He looks older."

I hesitated again. "He was in that graduate class I took last year as a PhD candidate."

"How old?" she repeated.

"Twenty-nine."

She considered this. "What's his last name again?"

"Chambers," I replied, praying she didn't recall my professors' names.

She smiled and sat back in her chair. "Maybe he'd like to join us for dinner later?"

"Mom, I've had an exhausting day. I'd really just like to go home, shower, and sleep when I get discharged.

Luckily, she agreed. But as soon as I was discharged, she drove me back to the sorority and then Stella took over nursing duty, even though I felt totally fine.

OWEN

It had physically pained me to see Bridget in that hospital bed. She appeared rather unaffected by the entire event, but I could barely close my eyes without being inundated with haunting visions of the firefighter carrying her out of the smoky building. And I couldn't help thinking what would have happened if they'd arrived five minutes later.

I knew what I should be focused on at the moment was my career, and how to salvage it, but all I could think is how none of it even mattered without Bridget.

I moved into a hotel while they tested the air quality throughout my apartment building. Only one unit had any notable damage, so the rest of us were assured we could return within a week, if not sooner. Bridget's mother stayed with her until her discharge Friday afternoon, and then Stella wouldn't let her out of her sight until Saturday afternoon. It was nearly dinner time when she drove to my hotel. I pulled her into the room as soon as she arrived, kissing her like I hadn't seen her in weeks.

"Mi spiace," I whispered, *I'm sorry*. "Ti amo. Sei tutto per me." *I love you. You're everything to me*, I told her.

Bridget nudged me backwards. "Owen, stop. You act like you could've lost me and it wasn't that big of a deal. They had the fire under control so even if they hadn't dragged me out when they did, I would've been fine. You have nothing to apologize for and you're just making me feel sad by harping on it. Okay?"

I nodded. The last thing I wanted was to make her feel worse. The adrenaline still coursing through my veins told me it had been a big deal, but I acknowledged in part that I might be focusing more on the relief of not losing Bridget to the fire in order to distract myself from the strong likelihood that I was about to lose her to the chaos and public criticism of our relationship.

She leaned forward, tentatively kissing me. I resisted for a moment, certain there was more for us to discuss, then acquiesced. Being with Bridget distracted me in a way nothing else could. She hibernated with me at the hotel the rest of the weekend, leaving briefly Sunday to collect more clothes and the books for her Monday classes.

When she left my bed Monday morning, the warmth I'd felt with her snuggled against me was quickly replaced with dread. Fortunately, I didn't have the luxury of sitting around worrying, as I had a full day of teaching and office hours.

As I approached my office, I half expected to see police tape, stacks of hate mail, or graffiti insults painted across the door. Instead, everything looked normal. I had no unusual voice mails or emails, nothing suggesting I was about to be fired for breaking the cardinal rule of teaching.

I went to my first class, teaching with an unease I hadn't felt in front of a class for years, then returned to my office, only to find there was still nothing out of the ordinary. I was too anxious to eat much for lunch, and I barely accomplished any grading, nervously watching the door anytime I heard footsteps in the hall.

Shortly before my second class, Professor Mancini dropped by.

My initial panic at his appearance wore off when I realized he was only there to offer his condolences about the fire. He casually asked if I was there when it happened, and when I told him I was not, he asked when I'd be able to move back in. The entire conversation was innocuous, so much so, in fact, that I actually relaxed and let me guard down as I taught my second class, then finished up my regularly scheduled office hours.

I knew I wasn't by any means in the clear yet, but the fact

that nothing had happened so far was unexpected and promising. As the clock moved to six, I texted Bridget, sharing my relief. Then I packed up my bag and headed out. I picked up dinner on the way back to the hotel, eating at the desk in the small room while watching TV.

Right when I finished, my phone rang. My gut clenched at the sight of the unfamiliar number and I swear my voice was shaking as I answered. It was my apartment superintendent phoning, telling me the fire department had given the all clear to my unit and I was welcome to move back in any time after eight AM the following morning.

As I hung up the phone, and started to feel relief, I noticed a new unread email. It was from the department head.

I swallowed the lump rising back in my throat as I read the message. It was formal and to the point, asking me to come to his office the next morning at 9 AM for a meeting with him and the Dean. He noted that Professor Mancini would cover my morning class.

I knocked my empty bowl and wrapper off the desk, swearing loudly. I knew what this email meant, and there was no point in delaying the inevitable.

I waited until the next morning before texting Bridget. I wished I could've let her remain oblivious longer, but obviously she'd notice my absence in class. Still, I tried to downplay the significance of the meeting, wishing that maybe the optimistic version of events I told her would prove true.

BRIDGET

I couldn't focus during any of my classes Tuesday after learning that Owen wouldn't be teaching Italian that morning. When I asked him for an update after class, he replied that I was not to worry and that I could call after class. I didn't follow either instruction.

When I rang his apartment doorbell right after my last class, Owen answered the door, looking haggard and surprised to see me.

"You shouldn't have come over here," he said, frowning.

He pulled me inside, peered out suspiciously, then slammed the door shut.

"I don't think it will help if anyone sees us together."

"Why? The damage is already done, isn't it?" I replied, realizing there was no chance his meeting had gone well.

Owen was practically sneering. I had never seen him look this distraught. He still had the acutely concerned expression he'd worn since the fire, but now it was overshadowed by the dark puffy circles beneath his eyes. There was only one thing that could've caused this much stress to him in a single day.

"Owen, I am so sorry," I said. I reached for him, but he pulled back.

"You have nothing to be sorry about, Bridget. I knew what I was doing and did it anyway. I'm the adult here, and I..."

"I am an adult too!" I interrupted, both annoyed and confused by his insistence. "Owen, you hardly took advantage of me. No one could possibly insinuate this isn't a consensual relationship. I knew you were off limits and I pursued you anyway."

I paused. "I have no regrets for me personally. Whatever happens to me, getting to be with you was worth it. I only wish I didn't screw things up so badly for you."

Owen pulled me to him and wrapped his arms so tightly around me that I could barely breathe. But despite the crushing sensation, it was wonderful. It was the most relief I'd felt in days. I didn't want him to let go. Ever. Luckily, he seemed to feel the same way, and he didn't let go.

When we finally parted, it was only so I could rise onto my toes to reach his mouth. The kiss was forceful and would've knocked me backwards, except Owen was holding me too tightly. I felt him smile against my mouth as I lost my balance, and he gently guided me upright. We found our way to the bed, both of us too upset to connect in any way but a physical one.

After, we must have laid there for a half hour before I garnered the courage to ask him about his meeting. It wasn't that I was afraid of his answer, just that I didn't want the peaceful embrace to end.

"We have to talk eventually," I said.

"No we don't," he replied. "Voglio solo pensare a te."

I only want to think of you, I translated silently with a smile. God it was distracting when he was so romantic in Italian. Especially when I was still staring at his perfectly sculpted bare chest. Despite his efforts, I persisted.

"So you met with the Dean and Professor Lazarro, right? What did they say? What did you say?"

He took a deep breath and slowly blew it out before speaking. "They said it had come to their attention that I may be involved romantically with a student in the Italian department. I said that I was, but that the relationship had just begun after the summer program in Italy ended and that we ended it as soon as I learned I would be your instructor again."

"Good. So there's no problem then, right?"

"Professor Lazarro remembered how I resisted accepting your class from Professor Rizzo's schedule and said that fact, combined with your presence in my apartment in the middle of the night, led them to think we were still involved romantically."

I winced. "Oh, God. How did you explain that?"

"I said you had a disagreement with someone in your

sorority and that I offered to let you sleep at my place since I was not there. The building records show my key card being used at the time of the fire, and they can tell from the security footage that it was actually me at my office at the time. They seemed to believe everything I told them, but they still had some concerns about me being involved with you at any time, even if not while I was your professor."

He paused. "They asked if there was any chance this could be construed as nonconsensual by any party involved."

"Owen, I'd never say that! You don't have to worry about that at all."

"I know, I know. I said that wasn't a concern, but that I was definitely the one to instigate the relationship."

I sat abruptly. "Why would you say that? You have way more to lose here than I do. Let them think I pursued you."

He shook his head. "Tesoro, it doesn't matter. I've read the policies a dozen times. No matter how I spin it, I broke the rules. But maybe you did not.""But if we just started dating this fall, you didn't break the rules. It's not your fault Professor Rizzo had surgery."

"I should've refused the appointment and told them why. If I'd just come forward, I don't think it would have been an issue."

"You said there was no one else to teach it. They didn't give you a choice!"

"It doesn't matter." He sighed and brought my hand to his lips. "Please don't worry about all this. Quel che sarà sarà."

I rolled my eyes. I didn't have a "what will be, will be" type of personality. No, I was a mover and a shaker. "So what's next? Did they decide anything?"

"Not officially. I get a formal hearing and investigation, unless I resign first. I've been placed on administrative leave pending the outcome of the investigation, which likely means for the rest of the semester."

"We'll fight it. My dad can recommend a good lawyer and when the hearing is over, they'll be apologizing to you for this whole mess."

Owen forced a half smile. "And then what? You need three Italian classes next semester. The department is too small for both of us."

"I can take all three with another professor. Or I can just take the minor in Italian. I don't need the major."

"You do for your award."

"I don't need the award. My parents paid my tuition and you know they'll pay for grad school, too."

"Even when they find out you were sleeping with your sleazy professor?" Owen asked, eyebrow cocked. "Besides, grad school is competitive and they don't let that many native English speakers into the French programs. That award gives you the edge you need to guarantee acceptance into your first choice program."

"I don't care. Sei tutto ciò che voglio."

Owen smiled broadly now. "You're everything I want too, biscottino."

"I got an email from Professor Lazarro asking me to emet with him and the Dean on Thursday," I said.

He nodded. "Yeah, they said they'd interview you as part of their investigation."

"I don't want to make things worse by saying the wrong thing."

"You'll do fine," he assured me. "But really, in the meantime, you probably shouldn't be seen coming and going from my apartment."

I sighed.

CHAPTER 20

BRIDGET

I attended all of my classes Wednesday and Thursday, grateful for any distraction at all. But it was impossible to concentrate in class Thursday, seeing Professor Mancini at the front of the room where Owen belonged. Owen made me promise not to visit him that evening, but I was eager to get home so I could at least call him.

As I packed up my books ready to make my exit, though, Professor Mancini motioned me towards his desk.

"I'd like to speak with you privately. Are you available to stay after class for a bit?"

I nodded nervously.

"Let's go to my office," he said. It wasn't exactly a request, so I figured I had no choice but to follow. It was only a few doors down from Owen's office, but significantly larger. Clearly, seniority had some benefits.

I sat in the chair facing his desk and waited as he closed the door behind him.

He sat, then frowned, breathing loudly. "I wanted to speak with you privately because I was informed that you are involved in an investigation within our department. Are you aware of this?"

I hesitated, then nodded.

"Are you familiar with the generalities of the issue?"

I nodded again.

Professor Mancini waited expectantly, then when it was clear I hadn't planned to continue, he said, "And?"

"I had a brief fling with Owen Chambers after the summer program in Italy, and even though it was over before the school year even began, I guess the department head is freaking out."

Professor Mancini's expression didn't change, so either he already knew the rumor was true or didn't particularly care. The silence made me nervous though, so I kept talking.

"I know they're investigating Owen now and I think it's ridiculous. He never did anything wrong or violated any of the university policies. I'm going to talk with the department head and dean later so we can get all this sorted out."

Professor Mancini frowned. "I don't think it is as simple as you've expressed. I believe they are investigating you as well. They've asked me about your performance in my class this semester and last spring."

I swallowed nervously, unsure of what to say.

"They have seen your transcripts, of course, and I assume your grades in other Italian classes are similar to those from mine," he continued.

"All As," I said. "In French and Italian."

He nodded. "I told them you were an excellent student. Your enthusiasm about the language is authentic and you are hard-working and focused."

"Thank you."

"They asked about your performance in class, whether your speaking skills and in-class writings are similar quality to assignments completed out of class too, though."

I frowned, perplexed as to why that would be an issue.

"Generally that is only something that arises if there is a concern that a student is cheating, that someone else may be assisting with assignments out of class."

My jaw dropped as I realized the implication. "Owen would never do my work for me!" I was offended that anyone even thought I would cheat, but then as I thought about it, I supposed Owen had edited papers for me or helped me with conjugations. And thanks to him, I could probably write a series of romantic Italian sonnets in my sleep.

"That was my impression of Mr. Chambers as well, and I don't see any distinction in the quality of work you complete in the classroom versus out of the classroom which would justify such an accusation. But I thought you should know."

"Thank you."

"I find you to be a promising Italian student and would like to see you succeed in our program here. There is a significant cultural difference that makes it difficult for me, having been raised the Italian way, to comprehend why your country focuses so intently on this sort of scenario. In Italy, people fall in love with coworkers, employers, professors, whoever. And it is not a problem. Here, there are all these rules."

He sighed. "But for whatever reason, the department is taking this investigation very seriously and I think you should as well. They have asked me to gather your old coursework, if you have it, and to review it for any irregularities. If they have any reason to believe any of your work is

FOR LOVE AND ITALIAN

not authentically yours, they will take away the credit for that course."

"Then I wouldn't have enough for the major," I said.

He nodded. "Yes. So I advise you take this investigation seriously. I shouldn't say this, but I wouldn't meet with them alone if I were you. They are just looking for a way to trap you. The university has some legal aid workers who may be able to accompany you, or at least offer some advice."

I swallowed the lump rising repeatedly in my throat. I knew exactly what I needed to do; I just didn't want to do it.

I tried to think of an alternative plan the entire walk back to my house, but of course, there was none. I waited until I was securely shut in my room at the sorority before dialing the familiar number.

"Yes," he answered his phone so briskly that I wasn't even sure it was him.

"Daddy?"

"Yes, Bridget. I'm at work. What is it?" His voice sounded distant and distracted. I envisioned him flipping through documents with me on speaker phone.

I took a deep breath. "I'm in trouble and I need help."

The phone clicked loudly and his voice was instantly clearer and full of concern. "What's wrong, Bridget? Are you okay?"

"Yes. I'm fine. I just, well, I think I might need some legal advice."

"You're not in jail, are you?" His voice was hushed now.

"No dad, I didn't commit a crime. I just, well, I guess I violated one of the university policies and now they're investigating and I don't know what to do."

"Hang on," he said. The line went silent for a moment. "Okay, I have a meeting in ten minutes, so just tell me exactly what happened so we know how to proceed. Do you know what policy they claim you violated?"

"Yes."

"And did you?"

"Well, yes, but…"

"Bridget, I don't believe this. You are so close to graduating. What were you thinking? Did you cheat on something?"

"No. I earned every single grade I've gotten, but the university is looking into all my Italian courses, and I think they're maybe going to take those off my transcript, and if they do that, I won't have enough for a major and I'll have to postpone graduation at least another semester and I'll lose my award."

He sighed. "Start at the beginning. What policy did you allegedly violate?"

"I can email it to you later. I don't know the exact wording, but I, um, I sort of went out with my Italian professor."

There was a lengthy pause, which I assumed to be as uncomfortable for my father as it was for me.

"Went out with, as in, dated?"

"Yes."

"One time?"

There were too many times to count. "I've been seeing him for almost a year," I finally said.

He was silent for several minutes.

"But what about the man your mother met at the hosp…" his voice trailed off. "Oh. That was your professor?"

"Yes."

"You were at your professor's house in the middle of the night and a fire broke out and now the university knows you were with him in the middle of the night?"

"Yes."

"Well I assume he's been fired?"

I swallowed hard. "Not yet."

He sighed with irritation. "Don't worry Bridget. The

university has no cause for penalizing you for this jerk taking advantage and if they even try…"

"Dad," I interrupted. "It's not Owen's fault. And I'm not going to say anything that will hurt him."

My father exhaled sharply, in a way that conveyed his feelings about the situation more than words ever could.

"He already spoke with the university officials conducting the investigation. He told them the relationship started at the end of summer after I was no longer in his class and that we ended it once we learned he'd be teaching me again. He told them he instigated it. He says they're going to fire him no matter what, but he worked so hard to get where he is that I can't make it any worse for him. He needs to be able to get another job as a professor somewhere."

Now my father snorted, clearly not concerned with Owen's career prospects.

"I thought that what he said, you know, telling them it didn't start until later, meant I would be safe, but my current Italian professor just told me that they've asked him about my coursework and my grades, so I think they're looking into all my work. They think Owen gave me an A in all of his classes because of our relationship, not because I earned them."

"It's a logical and fair assumption."

"But it isn't true. I get As in French too, and I'm getting an A in my current Italian class with another professor. I think I saved my exams and essays from his classes, too, so maybe another professor can review my work and agree that my grades were fair."

He sighed again. "Email me your transcripts, copies of all your current and past Italian coursework with the date and instructor stamped on it, and a copy of the policy they're charging you with violating."

"Okay," I said, jotting down a list.

"And I'll need to speak with your professor, of course."

"My current one?"

"Are you dating him, too?"

"No!" I tried to keep my breathing calm. "Why do you need to speak with Owen?"

"Bridget, do you want my help or not?" he snapped.

"Yes. I'll email everything to you."

"Okay. I'll look over everything and should be able to make it up to campus sometime next week but don't talk with anyone about this until then."

OWEN

The next several days were tense. I still wasn't permitted to teach my own classes, so I had nothing but worries to pass the time. I began to look for positions at other schools, but suspected my prospects would be limited until fall, at best. Bridget relayed what Professor Mancini had told her, and that she had involved her father. She said this apologetically, as though I'd be mad, but really, I was relieved.

We were in over our heads.

Her dad came to campus Friday morning, meeting alone with Bridget first, then chatting with Professor Mancini. When he arrived at my office, Bridget was at his side, but he quickly ordered her to wait in the hall.

She shot me a panicked grimace and shook her head. "Dad, I'm not going to wait in the hall like a child."

"It's fine, Bridget," I said, almost preferring the thought of being scolded without her watching.

I motioned for her father to come in and sit down, closing the door behind him. I took a deep breath before launching into my apology, but he dismissed me with a wave of his hand.

"I've got a full day here, and I'm not happy about missing

work as I have more than enough to keep me occupied there. So we can skip right over whatever explanations or excuses you have. I've reviewed the university policies and it's difficult for me to see where you could have been confused about the appropriateness of a relationship with my daughter when she was your student. Particularly as she was your significantly younger and less mature student, I might add. Bridget seems to think these rules shouldn't matter since you always graded her fairly regardless of your feelings towards her, but there are many other rational reasons for such rules. As a teacher, you hold a position of influence and power over your students, and whether or not you intend to exert that power, you are influencing your students."

He sighed, but didn't pause long enough for me to interrupt. "Bridget is legally an adult, but you should know from working with college students that the decision-making portions of the brain don't function the same way at twenty-one as they do later in life. Bridget is impulsive, and often irrational. We sent her to school assuming her professors would help her mature and become more independent, not to take advantage of her malleability."

He set a stack of papers in front of me. "I spoke with Mr. Mancini, and he looked at these assignments Bridget completed for your past classes. Based on that discussion, I've prepared this."

I read the paper he handed me. It was labeled Affidavit of Professor Edoardo Mancini. He said he had no personal knowledge of any improper relationship between me and Bridget, that he reviewed her work from classes I'd taught and agreed with all of the grades I'd assigned her. He also said that his assessment of her work in class was consistent with the grades she had received in other Italian classes.

I gazed up and nodded, unsure of the significance of that document.

"I appreciate you setting forth the timeline for the department head the way that you did, Mr. Chambers, as I don't see any validity to the university's threat to void the grades in any of Bridget's classes, aside from possibly her class that you taught this semester. I have prepared an affidavit for you to sign as well, but feel free to revise as needed for accuracy. I can have my office email over a new copy for you to sign before I meet with the dean and department head."

I swallowed, reading the affidavit he prepared for me. It of course contained inaccurate dates for the timing of my relationship with Bridget, but that was a lie I had begun, and which I clearly needed to maintain. The rest of it simply stated that her grades were an accurate reflection of her performance and that I had scored her in an unbiased fashion.

"This is fine," I said, my voice cracking.

He handed me an expensive looking pen, which I accepted. I poised my hand to sign, then paused.

"I think you should know I plan to resign."

Bridget's father was clearly pleased to hear this, but he attempted to mask his approval. "Bridget said you love teaching here."

"I do, very much so. But I don't see any outcome of this investigation that results in me still working as a professor here, and if that's the case, I might as well do whatever I can to make it easier to find a teaching position at a different university." I paused. "And Bridget really is a gifted Italian student and deserves the double major award, but if I were still here teaching, it would be difficult for her to fit enough classes from other professors in her schedule to complete the major."

His poker face returned, and he was quiet for much too long. "Does my daughter know you've made that decision?"

I shook my head. I'd planned to speak with her today, before I told the department head.

"And you want to leave, to teach somewhere else?"

I nodded again.

Mr. Williams pulled the pen out of my hand and began scrawling away on the paper, crossing out portions of the affidavit and adding other items. Then he flipped it over and wrote several sentences. He slid the paper back across the desk to me, face down.

"I have written a proposal for your resignation here. Essentially you admit no wrongdoing and offer to resign at the end of this semester on the condition that all notation of this investigation is removed from your file and you are given a positive reference for future employment. Mr. Mancini will finish the semester as the professor in Bridget's class but you will return to your other classes until the end of the semester." He paused and turned the paper over. "I've revised the affidavit accordingly."

I began to read his revisions, and everything looked fine. But it didn't make sense.

"Why would you help me?" I asked.

Mr. Williams cocked his head to the side. "I believe it is in Bridget's best interest for you to be at a different university as soon as possible. The fact that you also would like that is simply an added benefit."

I nodded. His explanation was blunt, but it made sense. And I didn't blame him. I knew what he saw when he looked at me.

"If this is acceptable to you, I'll send the revisions to my office and have them finalize both documents for you to sign and submit today. It would be wise for you to meet with your own attorney prior to signing anything though."

I read everything again, then shook my head. "No. This is fine."

He took the paper and stood, apparently calling his office. He read the new documents aloud, then thanked the listener and hung up. "The final versions will be emailed to you in a few minutes if you can print them."

"Sure." I exhaled, relieved. I glanced into the hall, where Bridget was chewing her fingernails. Her eyebrows were furrowed and her eyes were trained on her feet. I hated seeing how stressed I'd made her.

"Mr. Williams," I said, already dreading having spoken but knowing it needed to be said. "I am fully cognizant that what I did was wrong, and I have no excuse, but I did want you to know that Bridget is an exceptional young woman. I don't think she's irresponsible or immature and she's definitely not easily influenced."

I paused, half expecting him to punch me. "And I assure you I never meant to hurt her. I love Bridget and I want what's best for her."

His jaw visibly tightened, but he didn't speak. Instead, he glanced down at his phone. A moment later, he gazed up. "You should've received the email now. I'll wait in the hall while you review and sign."

CHAPTER 21

BRIDGET

*O*wen assured me my father hadn't pressured him to resign, but that was hard to believe. Owen was a fighter, and he loved this job. He wouldn't just abandon it if he had any other options. At this point though, it was done. The university accepted the terms of his resignation, so Owen was officially job hunting. He warned me that he was unlikely to find a position as a professor until the fall semester, but I actually thought that might be nice. That way we'd have more time together this spring and ideally I could head to grad school near wherever he would be teaching in the fall.

My dad also fixed the situation for me. As long as I received a C+ or greater in the class Professor Mancini took over from Owen, the university would count it as completion of the pre-requisite I needed for my remaining Italian classes. Neither the credits from that class nor the grade would go on my transcript, however, which meant I'd be three credits short of the Italian major. In other words, I'd be taking eighteen hardcore academic credits my last semester of college. That sucked, but was admittedly better than any of the other likely resolutions of the situation. I knew I owed my dad a huge thank you, but I had to do it via email since he wasn't exactly speaking to me now.

Owen thought we should keep our distance until the semester ended, which I understood. I didn't want to risk the university going back on any of its agreements, and there was no rush for us to spend every instant together now since we wouldn't have to hide anymore next semester. Besides, it was almost Thanksgiving. I was headed home the following Tuesday after classes, and when I returned, there would only be one week of classes before finals. I could survive that long.

Owen and I spoke on the phone Saturday night. I expected a long conversation about everything and nothing, running well into the early hours of the morning. But instead he was cold and distant. He said he was stressed out and tired, and that he needed some time to think.

I knew what that meant, but he assured me I was wrong. He said he loved me, that he didn't have to think about us but rather about his career.

Stupidly, I believed him.

I gave him the space he needed. I texted him Sunday to let him know I was thinking about him, but otherwise I totally backed off. Stella tried to keep my mind off him, but I wasn't in the mood to party with her. Besides, as much as she said she hadn't meant what she'd said back on the beach in August, I knew she did. She never understood my relationship with Owen. Plus, she'd believed from the start we'd get caught.

"You sure you won't even come out for dinner?" she asked Monday evening as she zipped her knee-high boots. "Nothing fancy, just some appetizers and drinks at Pete's."

I shook my head. As much as the small bar near campus sounded good to me most nights, tonight I wasn't in the mood. "Have fun. I'm going to start packing."

She hugged me then left reluctantly.

I checked my phone. Still nothing from Owen. I texted him.

"Hey, cutie. You busy tonight?"

He replied quickly, which was clearly a good sign. "Still thinking. Come over tomorrow before you leave town?"

I was bummed by his response, but agreed, turning my attention to packing instead.

I'd made decent headway when my phone buzzed again. I lunged at it, hoping Owen had changed his mind and wanted me to come over now, but it was a text from Stella instead.

"Owen's here," she said. "Bet you wish you came now."

I did, except I knew I shouldn't be seen in public with him anyway, so it was probably for the best. Although, I was a little resentful that he would head out to a bar when he claimed to be thinking. Not exactly the most meditative environment.

"Is he alone?" I texted back.

Her response took ages. I figured she was drinking and having a blast and not checking her phone often, which was understandable. Finally, she texted back.

"No. Looks like he's w his sister," she said.

Oh. Well, that actually did make sense. It was hard for me to understand siblings being so close since my brothers still acted like immature buffoons, but I couldn't deny the connection Owen and Olivia shared. If anyone could help him figure out his next step, it was her. I'd mentioned her to Stella before, since both of us were intrigued by the whole twin thing.

I returned to my packing, and my phone buzzed again. I

finished adding my remaining accessories, zipped up the bag, then turned to my phone.

It was another text from Stella. "You're right, she is cute," it said.

Right as I remembered she was talking about Owen's sister, another text came through from Stella. This one was a picture. It was blurry and taken from across the bar, but showed Owen at a table with a woman who was decidedly not Olivia.

My breath caught in my throat as I zoomed in closer, hoping maybe Olivia had just dyed her hair or something. But it was definitely not Olivia. As I stared at the photo, a lump formed in my stomach. That woman wasn't Olivia, but she was familiar. I was almost positive I'd seen a picture of that woman before and I would bet my undergraduate degree that it was Laura, his ex-girlfriend.

I took several deep breaths, harnessing everything I'd learned in all of the dumb yoga classes Stella had dragged me to. After a minute, I felt better. But then I glanced at my phone and saw that awful picture again and all the anger and stress flowed right back. I chucked my phone across the room, growling.

I reminded myself that he had been the one to end things with Laura, and that he had done so ages ago. I'd never been the possessive type, and it wasn't my place to control who he met for drinks.

Except he wasn't out for drinks. He was home, thinking. Or at least that was his story.

I scrambled for my phone, determined to help Owen redeem himself without him ever having to know that for a brief moment, I hadn't trusted him.

"Still thinking?" I texted Owen.

Next I texted Stella. "Is he still there? Does he look stressed?"

Stella wrote back first. "No, looks good. Currently laughing at something sis said. Guess she's a comedian."

I clenched my phone tightly, reminding myself that Stella's answer alone meant nothing. Any moment now Owen was going to reply that he'd given up on thinking and headed out to a bar and just ran into his ex. Or maybe he wouldn't reply at all now and he'd tell me everything tomorrow.

I prepared to wait all night, but within a minute, I had my answer.

"Yes. Planning on early bedtime," Owen wrote. "See you tomorrow. Love you."

I glanced from my phone to my already-packed bag. I could storm down to the bar and embarrass myself and Owen, cry myself to sleep tonight, then stress all throughout Italian class tomorrow. Or I could take this as a sign and head home tonight.

I took option B.

OWEN

I felt better when I awoke Tuesday morning. I'd already plotted out my possible career paths from this point, but actually running the options by someone else at a similar point in the world of higher education helped. Now I just needed to talk to Bridget. I felt terrible not telling her where I had been the night before, but in light of who I'd been with, I wanted to tell her in person. Bridget wasn't the jealous type. I knew that. But still…

I sent her a text as her Italian class should've been wrapping up. She didn't reply, but I figured she was packing. After her next class, I texted again.

"Indian or Thai?" I asked.

No response.

Twenty minutes later when I still hadn't heard back, I called. Bridget didn't answer.

I waited a little longer, then tapped out another text. "If you don't answer in five minutes, I'm ordering extra spicy red curry."

This time, her response was immediate.

"Went home early," she said. "Looks like I need to do some thinking of my own."

My mouth grew dry as I pondered this. She'd been fine when we last spoke, so something must have happened during class.

"What happened?" I wrote.

"You know."

I rolled my eyes. Had I known, I wouldn't have asked. Obviously.

I hated games like this where I was apparently supposed to guess the right answer. There was never a winner.

"Call me," I said.

"No. I can't do this now. I need time to think."

I frowned. There was a ringing in my ears and my pulse raced. Clearly something had happened and Bridget was upset. But what? Or why?

"What changed?" I asked.

"You," came her response. "We'll talk after the break. Have a good Thanksgiving."

I clenched my teeth together so hard I tasted blood.

CHAPTER 22

BRIDGET

*H*eading home early was exactly what I needed. The change of scenery distracted me from Owen. Plus, being Thanksgiving, there was comfort food aplenty. As had become tradition the night before the holiday, I hit the local bars with some other high school alumni. My mom asked if Owen would be meeting up with us and when I informed her we didn't need to mention him anymore, she did her best to hide her glee.

Owen texted often, "checking in," as he called it. He even had the nerve to email and act like he had no clue what was upsetting me. Thanksgiving was harder, with no one but my immediate family to distract me. Friday was spent shopping, followed by a quick nap. Mid-afternoon, I was in the kitchen baking with my mom. We were making cranberry lemon scones, so the entire house smelled fantastic.

My brothers' friends had been coming and going all day,

so when the doorbell rang, I thought nothing of it. Michael paused the video game and went to the door.

I nearly dropped the tray of lightly browned pastries when I heard Owen's voice. I strained to hear my brother's response, but there was nothing. I slid the second tray into the oven and shut the door right as Michael appeared around the corner.

"There's some guy here to see you," he said with complete disinterest.

"Tell him I don't want to see him right now."

"Tell him yourself," my brother replied with an eye roll, collapsing back onto the couch and resuming his game.

I glanced over at my mother, who was doing her best to pretend she was fully engrossed in the cookbook. Blowing out a sigh, I yanked off my apron, smoothed a hand over my hair, and went to the foyer.

Owen was still outside, even though the door was wide open. He was facing the sizable front lawn, dotted with patches of well-manicured flowers, so his back was to me. I contemplated shutting the door and just walking away, but he turned suddenly. He had two days worth of stubble and his eyes suggested he hadn't slept much in as long, but my heart still fluttered when I saw him.

This was my problem with ridiculously hot guys like Owen. Even when my heart ached and my brain told me to hate him, my hands still longed to touch every inch of his perfect body. I dropped my gaze before I got lost in his fiercely blue eyes.

"You're at my house," I blurted out, sounding ridiculous. To ensure I could resist the urge to invite him in brought on by my overly formal upbringing, I stepped down onto the porch and pulled the door shut behind me.

"I didn't know what else to do. You wouldn't talk to me."

"I'm sorry you wasted a trip, but I have nothing to say to you."

He frowned, fidgeted with his hands, then shoved them into the pockets of his khakis. "Bridget, I don't even know what I did to upset you." His voice was soft, but pleading.

I swallowed. More than anything, I wanted him to be able to explain away what Stella saw, to convince me I hadn't completely misinterpreted what I thought we shared, but I knew he couldn't. And the more opportunity I gave him to do so, the more likely I was just to get sucked back in. Owen Chambers was not the man I thought he was, and no matter how convincing and romantic he came off when he spurted out his heart-melting Italian one-liners, it wasn't real.

"Owen, really, you should go."

He stared back at me, his sapphire eyes filled with disbelief, but he didn't budge. After what felt like an eternity, he shuffled his feet and glanced side to side as though he were considering leaving. But then he turned back to me.

"I'm not leaving until you tell me what's going on, Bridget."

I bit back tears. "You can do whatever. I'm going back inside now."

"I lost my fucking job for you, Bridget!"

The volume and passion of his words stopped me in my tracks.

"You seriously don't think you owe me any explanation?"

I took a deep pained breath before speaking. "Owen, I'm sorry. If I could get you your job back, I would."

"I don't want the job," he said. "I want you."

It took all of my willpower not to launch myself into his arms as he spoke. He seemed so sincere.

"Then why did you lie?" I finally asked.

He cocked his head to the side, imitating genuine confusion well.

"Where were you Sunday night?" I asked.

Owen peered towards the sky as he thought, and then, all at once, recognition washed over him. "You mean when I was with Laura?"

I nodded. "You said you needed time to think."

"I did."

I rolled my eyes. "Oh come on, Owen."

"I told you I needed time to think because I needed to figure out the next step. Bridget, I have to find a new job now, and that means I need a new place to live. And trying to decide all of that without knowing what your plans are next year or where you'll be is hard."

"So you thought your ex could help you figure that out? Wouldn't it have made more sense to just talk with me about my plans?"

"No, because I don't want you to revolve your plans around me. I want to be with you, but I've already screwed up your future enough. I needed someone outside of the situation to give me some unbiased feedback. And honestly? I wasn't ready to go out in public with you near campus where everyone is already talking. You really think people seeing us together will make any of this easier?"

There was so much wrong with his spiel that I didn't know where to begin. "Owen, come on. Do you hear yourself?"

He pouted. "I should have told you I was going out with Laura, but things were so tense with us last week and I didn't want to risk starting an argument. I didn't think you would see us and I guess I assumed if you did, that you'd come talk to me rather than assume the worst."

"I didn't see you," I said. "Stella did."

"Well I don't know what she told you, but we just had dinner and drinks. It wasn't a date. We are just friends now. Not even friends, really. But she knows me and my history and I figured she might have some insight on our situation."

"And did she?"

Owen breathed a laugh. "Unintentionally, yes."

I raised an eyebrow.

"She was shocked that I ever got involved with a student. She had heard the rumors and assumed it was a big misunderstanding and that you had seduced me or drugged me to get me into bed with you. She showed up feeling all sympathetic for me."

I tried not to grimace at the thought of his perfect ex-girlfriend trying to comfort him.

"So she was really surprised when I explained that it wasn't like that at all and that I was pretty sure you were the love of my life."

"You told her that?"

"I did." He paused. "Well, and she guessed it, sort of. She and I were together over a year, so even though we haven't seen each other much in the last two years, she still knows me better than a lot of people. It was pretty obvious to her how I feel about you, just from hearing me talk about you."

I pulled my arms closer around my body, trying not to shiver.

Owen reached for me, then hesitated. "Can I touch you? You're freezing."

I nodded, and he began rubbing his hands along my arms.

"I just need a minute to process all this," I said. "I was already struggling with everything that happened with the investigation, and then midterms, and then I learn you're meeting up with your ex behind my back, and…it's just a lot to take in."

Owen nudged me closer and wrapped his arms around me. "I'm sorry for sneaking around. I swear to you nothing happened with Laura. I should've just told you the truth, but in my twisted little brain I thought that would just compli-cate things. And I had no idea that was why you were ignoring me. I assumed it was something about the inves-tigation."

The slightest part of me suspected I shouldn't just accept his explanation, but in my heart, I knew he was telling the truth. And being fully enveloped by his arms felt too good.

"I missed you so much," he whispered, his warm breath tickling my ear.

"Me too. Ti amo."

"That's my line."

"No, you can do much better than that."

Owen kissed my forehead then pulled back slightly. "Sei tutto per me. Senza di te non posso più vivere."

You are everything to me. I can't live without you.

I started to say something, but he shook his head.

"I'm not done yet," he protested. "Non sono niente senza di te. Per te farei di tutto. Il mio cuore è solo tuo."

I am nothing without you. I'd do anything for you. My heart is yours.

I sighed, my insides officially having turned to mush.

Owen tilted my chin up to face him. "You are everything I want," he said, his eyes locked on mine.

I leaned in to kiss him before even registering that he'd actually spoken that last line in English. And here I'd thought he was only romantic in Italian.

Owen ended the kiss way too soon, clearing his throat and nodding towards the large picture window in the dining room.

"We have an audience," he whispered.

I turned to see David and Michael gawking from the window.

"Crap," I muttered.

Owen chuckled. "You should get inside before you freeze to death."

I frowned. I felt like I'd just gotten him back, so I really didn't want him to leave yet. "Can you stay?"

"When you wouldn't take my calls, I literally just packed my bags and drove out here without a plan. So yeah, I can stay as long as you want. Or until your dad chases me off the premises with a carving knife."

I squeezed his hand and then led him inside.

My brothers didn't even attempt to pretend they hadn't been gawking. I was suddenly embarrassed and grateful to Owen for cutting the kiss off before it got too out of hand.

"Owen these are my baby brothers, David and Michael. And this is Owen Chambers."

"Mike," he corrected, offering his hand to Owen.

David sniggered but shook Owen's hand as well.

An awkward silence ensued.

"So you're the Italian professor," Mike said.

Owen nodded warmly. "Do either of you speak any Italian?"

They both shook their heads.

"It's not even offered at the high school," I explained.

"Well, if you ever want to learn, I can teach you," Owen said.

"I'm not sure we have what it takes to succeed in your class," David said, laughing hysterically.

"David!" I glared at my brother, humiliated, before turning to Owen, who, thankfully, took the joke better than I did.

"Let me give you a tour," I said, motioning for Owen to follow me. The house had a fairly traditional floor plan, with a formal sitting room off the foyer and an office just past that. I led Owen to the other side, cutting through the dining room to reach the kitchen, where my mom was peering into the oven.

"You didn't set the timer," she said, turning as she spoke and paling at the sight of Owen. "Sorry, I didn't realize we had company."

"Mom, you remember Owen, right?"

She smiled politely. "Yes, of course. It's nice seeing you again."

"You have a beautiful home," Owen said.

"Thank you. Will you be joining us for dinner?"

"We hadn't really talked about our plans yet," I answered for him.

Owen glanced uncomfortably at me. "Could I use your restroom?"

I nodded and pointed down the hall, nestled between the laundry room and mudroom. Then I turned back to my mother.

"Why didn't you tell me he was coming?" she asked.

"He surprised me. Long story. But is it okay if I invite him to stay?"

"For dinner?"

"For the weekend," I said. "In the guestroom, of course," I added.

My mother looked panicked. "Honey, I don't know. Can I check with your dad? It's…you've never had a boyfriend stay over at the house. I'm not sure we're ready for that, and I don't know how your dad feels about Owen right now."

"I think Dad needs to get to know him better."

My mom sighed and glanced over to the bathroom. "Maybe so. I thought you two had broken up, though. Wasn't that why you came home early?"

I shook my head. "It was a misunderstanding."

"Well, honey, wouldn't it be wise to take some time to think about everything?"

I rolled my eyes. "We need to have this talk later. Owen can't pretend to be using the bathroom all day."

"He can at least stay for dinner," she said. "I'll talk with your father about the rest."

Owen returned, approaching slowly in case we were still discussing him, and I dragged him upstairs under the guise of finishing the house tour. Our first stop was my bedroom.

"So this is where you grew up," Owen said, gazing around my room.

I pulled the door shut. "For the last fifteen years."

"Are you allowed to have boys in your room with the door shut?" he asked with a grin, sitting on my bed.

I sat beside him. "Oh, so now you're all about following the rules?"

Owen laughed until I straddled his lap and kissed him. He responded in kind, again ending it long before I was ready.

"What's our plan here?" he asked.

I raised an eyebrow.

"I didn't have a formal agenda when I came here, I just knew I needed to see you. I don't want to intrude on your time with your family, and I get the distinct impression they're not thrilled about my presence here right now. I assume there is a hotel somewhere nearby I can stay at tonight, or I can drive back, but I should probably decide soon."

"Don't leave," I begged. "You just got here."

"Your parents…"

"Are insane," I interrupted. "They need to get to know you. Sooner or later, they will have to accept that you are a part of my life."

"Does that mean you're contemplating keeping me around long term?"

I smiled at the thought. "Speaking of long term, what are we doing next semester?"

Owen scooted me off his lap. "You are finishing your degree, earning your double major and linguistic awards and applying for grad schools. That is not up for discussion."

I already knew that was his position, and it wasn't like I had other options at this point anyway. I rephrased my question. "What are you doing next semester?"

He pushed off the bed and began to pace around the room. "I still don't know. There is a possibility a university somewhere might have a semester-long opening because of a maternity leave or early retirement. But I really only have one firm offer so far."

I didn't understand why he phrased this like a bad thing. For a sudden departure mid-year, even with a neutral letter of reference, it would raise flags on his applications. I knew he'd find something eventually, but I'd been worried it wouldn't happen until fall.

"That's wonderful. Owen, I told you that you were irresistible."

He smiled, but it wasn't genuine.

"Okay, so what's the caveat? You don't like that university? Crappy town?"

Owen shook his head. "No, it's a perfect job, ideal for a semester, gorgeous campus. It's just too far from you."

I tried not to pout openly. Especially after everything Owen had sacrificed to be with me, I was not going to hold him back when a good opportunity came his way. "Nothing is too far from me. We'll talk and text and video chat all the time. And I'll come visit you weekends. It's my last semester. I'm not going to have tons of homework so…"

"It's too far to drive."

"Then I'll fly," I said, needing to convince myself as much as him that it would work. I rose to my toes and kissed him.

He kissed me back briefly. "It's back in Florence."

"Florence, Italy?"

"Yes."

"Oh. The same university as this summer?"

"Yes."

I sighed. That made sense. And actually I could see how that would be a fantastic opportunity for him. But damn. That was far.

"I'm still looking closer to home, babe. Don't worry."

It took me a minute to garner the strength to say the next sentence aloud, but I did it. "You should go to Italy if that's what you want."

Owen frowned, which flustered me since he was supposed to recognize my loving gesture. Wasn't that an expression, that when you really love something, you set it free?

"You don't mean that," he said finally.

"How can you be so sure?"

He kissed the tip of my nose. "Because I know you."

"I already screwed up one job for you. I am not going to be responsible for you missing out on this chance."

"It's only one semester. It won't be the end of the world if I don't teach at all. I'll get back on track next fall."

I shook my head. "It's only one semester, so it won't be the end of the world if you do teach in Florence. We will make it work, Owen." I paused. "Just no meeting ex-girl-friends without telling me."

He laughed and pulled me close for a kiss.

"What is the schedule like there?" I asked.

"Their semester starts early. I'd have to go there right after Christmas, but I'd love if you could come with me."

I nodded, focusing on keeping the smile plastered on my face and remembering to breathe while feeling all the air being sucked out of the room.

"You don't start until mid-January, so we could have a good two weeks together," he said, sounding way too chipper. "Then our spring break is the last week of February, so I could fly back to see you for a week, and you could come back out to Italy over your spring break a couple weeks later. And of course I'll be back in time to see you graduate. Exams there are mid-April and grades are due by the 23rd."

I felt myself relax as he spoke. It wasn't just the fact that it did seem feasible to visit each other often despite the distance and the cost that perked me up. Mostly it was the fact that he was so certain he'd still want to see me all those times. Sure he'd said he'd never get enough of me, usually during (or immediately preceding or following) sex, or when he was speaking Italian to me. But seeing his actual plans to include me in his future was a whole different ballgame.

Before I knew what was happening, I was crying.

Owen dropped to his knees in front of me. "Mio cuore, what's wrong?"

I sniffled, then tried to explain it all.

His kissed my hands tenderly. "Bridget, when will you understand? All I want is you. I can figure the rest out, but I have to have you by my side."

OWEN

Sitting down to dinner with the entire Williams family was uncomfortable, to put it lightly. Mrs. Williams kept sneaking furtive glances at me, her eyes then darting back to her daughter. Mr. Williams was snarling at me like I was a pedophile. I kept my focus on the food, which was surprisingly tasty. My family had always eaten leftovers the day after Thanksgiving, but Bridget's mom had made some beef and noodle dish, a salad, and green beans.

"So I suppose you'll be busy packing up your office and apartment after the holiday," Mr. Williams said suddenly, his brow furrowed.

"Dad!" Bridget chastised.

"Well he's headed somewhere else for next semester, right?" her father responded.

I opened my mouth to say nothing had been finalized, but Bridget beat me to the punch. "He's been offered a prestigious professorship in Italy," she said proudly.

My fork slid out of my hand, hitting the plate with a loud CLANG.

"Oh, is that right?" her mother asked, suddenly cheerful and approving.

I cleared my throat awkwardly, dabbing at the food my fork had splattered on my pants. "Yes, although I haven't accepted the position yet."

Bridget squeezed my thigh and smiled. "But you're going to, right?" She turned back to her parents. "It's a great opportunity for Owen."

Her father smiled widely. "Indeed, it sounds tremendous."

BRIDGET

I'd never thought my brother would be the one to spare me an awkward dinner conversation, but right as my father launched into Owen, goading him about accepting the position in Italy, David interrupted.

"I've never really heard anyone speak Italian. Are you fluent?" he asked Owen.

"Sì." Owen replied.

"What about my sister? Is she fluent?"

Owen grinned and turned to me. "She can read it fluently and understands native speakers but occasionally mixes in some French in her writing and isn't quite conversationally fluent."

I laughed, having known he would say that.

"So can you say something in Italian? I mean, like more

than a word or two? I want to hear what it sounds like," David continued.

Owen hesitated. "None of you understand any Italian?"

I felt my cheeks begin to blush immediately, knowing he was going to say something ridiculous after confirming they wouldn't understand anyway. I braced myself for the worst.

He turned to me. "Tu sei la mia stella. Mi fa perdere la testa. Cara mia, ti voglio tanto bene. Vorrei annegare nei tuoi occhi."

It all sounded beautiful. And as he spoke, *You are my star. You make me lose my mind. My darling, I love you.* But when he reached the last sentence and said "I want to drown in your eyes," I couldn't help but giggle, which was the exact reaction he had hoped for.

"It is a beautiful language," my mother agreed.

"What's the translation?" my dad asked.

"Blah blah blah, then something about drowning," I said.

Owen shot me a bemused look. "Nothing too interesting, unfortunately. I just told Bridget that I'm fond of her."

Michael's eyes narrowed. "Umm am I the only one who definitely heard the word for balls? Testes. He definitely said testes."

David laughed and I rolled my eyes.

"Testa," I said. "It means 'brain,' as in 'you have a very small brain.'"

CHAPTER 23

BRIDGET

The next month of my life was evenly divided between school and Owen. If I wasn't in class or cramming for finals, I was with Owen. I had hoped by spending every possible moment with him, I'd finally get my fill of him. My plan backfired, though, as I suffered through a bout of withdrawal during the week we were separated for the holidays. Never before had I been so dependent on a man, and I hated it. I felt weak and pathetic, but so, so happy.

We spent New Year's Eve in Italy, making love so passionately that I nearly blacked out. When Owen began working two days later, I busied myself exploring the town, reading Shakespeare on a bench on a cobblestone street looking out over Ponte Vecchio, and people watching in the Piazza della Signoria. Each evening, Owen and I strolled through our neighborhood, talking and kissing at cafés over dinner, sampling different flavors of gelato, or snuggling on park benches. We ended each evening making love then falling asleep with our limbs still entwined.

I left paradise after eleven days, already calculating the hours until Owen would come visit near the end of February. I missed him so much that my heart literally ached, but I ignored the pain and by the second week of school, it had dulled significantly. We spoke when we could, but between the time change and our busy schedules, it was tough. Owen compensated for this by writing me long love letters, via email, of course, and it proved highly satisfying to draft my own equally passionate replies.

Thanks to the extra Italian class, my schedule was grueling, but enjoyable. Half of my classes were in Italian and the other half, French. When I wasn't studying or composing notes of my undying love for Owen, I researched graduate programs in French. Money being no object, I took the approach of applying anywhere even remotely appealing, knowing Owen was following an equally wide radius for his job search. With any luck, we'd end up at the same school or at least different schools in the same town.

When I had any free time, I spent it with Stella or my sorority sisters, partying and enjoying life as a second semester senior. Life was good.

OWEN

The first six weeks of classes flew by, and before I knew it, I was back with Bridget. I had sublet my apartment, and I couldn't very well stay in her sorority while I visited, so we spent the week in a hotel. It certainly lacked the romantic appeal of my Tuscan studio apartment, but any time I got to spend with Bridget was worthwhile. I had hoped to have nearly the full week to spend with Bridget, but I had scheduled interviews with another Midwestern university and with one in Boston, leaving Bridget and I only four days.

On the date I was scheduled to fly back to Italy, I had planned an extra stop. Finding out Bridget's father's phone number had been easy enough, after his involvement in the university investigation, but garnering the courage to call and ask to meet with him and his wife had been a challenge.

I arrived at their house a few minutes early, and Mr. Williams offered me a drink. Normally, I'd abstain since I was trying to make a good impression on him, but between the anxiety about the flight and my uncertainty at how he'd respond to my news, I was a nervous mess and figured a drink could only help.

"Sure, whatever you're having is great," I said, feigning confidence.

He reached for the whiskey. "Barbara told you Bridget isn't here now, right?"

I nodded. "Yes. I actually wanted to speak with both of you alone."

"I thought you were in Italy for the semester," Barbara said, entering the room and sitting down.

"I am. It's spring break at the university there, so I came back to see Bridget. I'm actually headed to the airport shortly."

"Please have a seat," Barbara said as her husband handed me my drink.

I thanked him and sat.

"That's a long flight for such a short visit," Mr. Williams said.

"It's three flights altogether," I said, sipping my drink. "But, um, it's worth it."

"Were you back here for interviews?"

"I had two, but I'll line up some more for summer. This trip was primarily to see Bridget."

They exchanged a glance.

I needed to get to my point before I lost my nerve. "Anyway, that's actually why I wanted to see you both. I know we didn't get to meet each other under the best of circumstances, and I wish, um, I would've handled things differently. But I really do care about your daughter. I love her, and I think I can make her happy. So I wanted to ask for your blessing to propose."

"To propose marriage?" Bridget's mom asked, wide-eyed.

"Yes."

"To Bridget?" she followed up.

I nodded. We all took a long swig of our drinks. I was starting to wish I could just disappear. This was a dumb idea. I knew they'd never approve, so why had I even bothered?

Bridget's dad shook his head. "Do you propose to all of your former students?"

I tightened my stomach. "Bridget is the only student I've ever been involved with, and the only woman I've ever wanted to marry." I paused. "I understand why you don't like me, and if she were my daughter I'd probably have the same reservations, but I can assure you I want to do right by her."

"So you agree it was wrong to date your student?"

I wondered if that was a trick question. I suddenly pitied any witness he'd ever interrogated on the stand. "I know it was against university policy, and I was well aware of that at that time. But if you're asking if I'd go back and do things differently, the answer is no."

Her dad snorted.

"Didn't you lose your job?" Barbara asked, as though there were some way I could've forgotten that major life changing event.

"Yes, but if I had to choose between my job and Bridget, I'd pick her every time."

This answer seemed to appease them. Their expressions softened and they sipped more slowly now.

"I don't mean to hurt your feelings," Barbara finally said, "But I just don't think Bridget is ready for marriage."

"She's not as old as you," her dad chimed in.

"She's pretty mature for her age," I said. "And it's not like we'd have to get married right away."

"Then why not wait to ask her?"

"Because I'm certain now that she's the person I want to spend the rest of my life with, and I want her to know that now. If she isn't there yet, that's fine. I'll wait for her as long as I have to."

Mrs. Williams opened and shut her mouth several times before finally speaking. "Bridget can be a very passionate person, and she's always been very good at getting people to like her. And she tends to get sort of swept up in things, so to speak, but then she eventually moves on. She just tends to flit from one passion to the next."

I waited, unsure of what she was trying to say.

"What I mean is that I suspect Bridget does really care for you now, but her feelings are so fleeting. Right now she just adores French and Italian and travel and you, of course. But a few years before that it was tennis, and a few years from now she might decide art is her new passion. And sometimes, Bridget does things just to prove to everyone that she can."

I drained my drink, pretty sure the woman I'd hoped to be my future mother-in-law just said she considered me to be a hobby for her daughter. It pained me to hear her think so little of Bridget or her ability to be serious about anything.

"I appreciate your concern but I don't think it is warranted. Bridget can definitely be impulsive, but she's also very dedicated and thoughtful, not flighty. I don't think 'land a professor' was on her bucket list, if that's what you're suggesting. She's a smart and capable woman and she knows who she is and what she wants."

I paused, feeling more confident now. "I'm pretty sure she feels the same about me as I do about her, but if not, I trust her to tell me. And if she agrees to marry me, there's not a doubt in my mind that she's in it for the long haul." I stood awkwardly.

"How will you support her?" she continued, unswayed by my clear attempt to escape. "You have no permanent job, and even if you do find another one, it would hardly pay for your grad school loans or her tuition, let alone all the traveling she seems to want to do now. Bridget has expensive tastes. She's used to designer clothes and frequent spa trips. And what if she wants kids? How would you ever afford them?"

I blew out a sigh. This woman was tough. And here, I'd thought Bridget's dad would be my bigger challenge. "I'll be teaching this summer and will have a full professorship somewhere by fall," I began, praying I could make it true by then. "I don't have any loans from school. I paid my tuition by working and teaching as I went. I'll make enough money to support her and pay for her school if need be, but as of now, she really wants to work as a teacher herself someday."

I paused again and they both exchanged glances as though I was the fool for thinking Bridget would ever work. Clearly they never saw how hard she pushed herself in school or how much dedication it had taken for her to add the Italian major and still graduate on time. "And she does want kids. Two. She says she'd like twins so they can be close like my sister and me."

I forced a smile and briefly looked them each in the eye. "Sorry for taking up your time, and thanks for the drink. I need to head out to the airport now."

I started towards the front door. Her dad followed.

"When do you plan to ask her?" he wanted to know.

"She'll be in Italy over her spring break in a couple weeks."

He glanced over to his wife.

"Well, uh, keep us posted, I guess. It's her decision, not ours. She could certainly do worse."

I wasn't sure what to make of that comment, so I thanked him and left.

CHAPTER 24

BRIDGET

*S*pring break took forever to arrive, but it was worth the wait. I arrived on Saturday, so Owen and I spent the weekend getting reacquainted in his small apartment. During the week, I sat in on his morning classes, then explored the city in the afternoon. In the evenings, we spent hours walking around the city hand in hand, tossing about possible options for our work/school the next year.

After Owen's Friday morning class, we took the train to Venice. My flight back to the States left Sunday, so I wasn't totally sure of the logic behind such a short excursion, but Owen promised it would be worth my while. It was only a two hour train ride, and I could never say no to Venice.

On Friday afternoon, we explored the romantic church of Santa Fosca. It was on its own tiny island called Torcello. Then we went to a quaint restaurant and ate beside a crackling wood fireplace. As if the night could possibly get more romantic, we then wandered Piazza San Marco.

"It's gorgeous here," I murmured, mesmerized by the way the light from the torch-style street lamps danced off the water. Everything looked serene and picturesque, just like in the movies. We could hear trills of live music coming from the square, but near us, it was quiet.

"I'm a little sad to not have an excuse to come back here after tomorrow," I added.

Owen chuckled, wrapping his arms loosely around me, his hands against my lower back. "You want me to stay on an extra year so you have more reason to travel?"

"No! That's not even funny," I said, smiling at the sparkle in his bold blue eyes. "But I do think I'd like to come back here again sometime with you."

He nodded. "There are a lot of places I want to explore with you eventually."

"Like where?"

"Well, for starters, France. We've barely scratched the surface there. And what about the rest of Western Europe?"

I frowned, trying to calculate how many extravagant international trips I'd even be able to afford on a graduate student budget. "It might take a while to explore the entire continent," I finally said.

"We have time. We could do it even if it takes a lifetime."

I started to reply, but stopped myself. Even though he probably wasn't trying to be romantic, the fact that he referenced a lifetime of travels with me made my insides feel all warm and tingly.

"There is nothing I want more than to spend the rest of my life exploring the world with you," he continued. "Once I'm back in the States, I want to wake up next to you every morning for the rest of my life."

"That's a long time," I said, feeling confused by his sudden romanticism. "Don't you think you'll get sick of me?"

Owen grinned wider and shook his head slowly side to

side. "I could stare into those gorgeous green eyes of yours for hours every day until I die and it still wouldn't be enough." He leaned forward and kissed me. His mouth pressed gently against mine and pulled away far too soon.

"And I could kiss your soft lips all day every day and never get my fill."

Suddenly, I realized what was throwing me about his sweet talking. "Hey, you're being romantic in English. Usually you only say these things to me in Italian."

Owen smiled again and I leaned forward, unable to resist kissing him. But he held me at bay with his hands pressed firmly against my hips and locked his eyes on mine. "You're very observant, tesoro mio. I am speaking English to you and it is completely intentional."

I raised an eyebrow.

"I have something very important to say to you tonight and I don't want to risk any confusion in translation," he asked. "But if you could stop interrupting, cuore mio, I was just about to say that your smile is contagious. And when I hear you laugh, I can't help but feel happy no matter how terrible my day has been."

He paused, and this time I didn't interrupt. The words themselves may not sound as romantic as in Italian, but I was still swooning.

"There are a lot of unknowns still in my future and I can't predict where I'll be in ten years, or even in five years, but I know I want you by my side wherever I am. You are my soul mate, and I love you."

Owen kissed me again, and this time it was much firmer and much quicker than before. By the time I registered his lips having left mine, he had gripped my hands in his and dropped to his knee on the cobblestone street.

"Mi vuoi sposare? Will you marry me?"

My heart thudded uncontrollably and I suddenly felt very warm and dizzy. I wanted to freeze this moment, to somehow record it forever so I could always remember how sweet and handsome and perfectly sexy Owen looked kneeling before me. I chastised myself for not realizing where he was headed with all this sweet talk beforehand and wished I was the kind of person who could think of some uber romantic response on the spot rather than just gawking at him, smiling.

Finally, the words came to me. Without a doubt, this was the man I wanted to spend my life with. "Si. Voglio invecchiare con te." *Yes. I want to grow old with you.* I paused, then added, "Yes."

Owen's smile broadened as he rose to his feet and swept me into his arms, hugging me so tightly that he lifted me off the ground. I felt my shoe slip off my foot and heard applause and cheering from across the street, but as my future husband kissed me, holding me tight in his arms, I didn't have a care in the world.

This time, I was the one to end the kiss, but only because I worried I was getting too heavy for Owen to hold much longer. He helped me back into my shoe and then sighed happily.

"I love you," I said, suddenly aware that people were still gawking at us.

Owen reached his hand into the pocket of his jacket. "I almost forgot," he said, opening a small velvet box and presenting it to me.

My eyes widened with glee. The box held a truly gorgeous and unique ring. There was a small but sparkling diamond in the middle, flanked on all sides by even tinier diamonds forming a vintage-style circle. The white gold band had a twisted vine design accented with vibrant emeralds. It was nothing like the engagement ring I ever expected to receive and yet it was absolutely perfect in every way. I couldn't imagine a more fitting ring.

"I thought about buying you a ring back home, but decided it made more sense to find one I liked in Italy. It felt more meaningful that way, and more unique. And this particular ring, well it just spoke to me." Owen paused and gazed up from the ring. "If you don't love it we can choose a different one. It won't hurt my feelings."

I would've laughed at his silliness but I was biting my lip to try to keep the tears at bay. "Babe, I adore it. This is the most amazing ring I have ever seen in my entire life." I rose to my toes impatiently. "Now hurry up and put it on me."

Owen slipped the ring onto my finger and we both exhaled the breath we'd been holding as the ring fit securely in place. I stared down at the ring, unable to look away.

"Where did you find this?"

"Ponte Vecchio."

"Wow. A gorgeous ring from the gorgeous city of Firenze given to me by the most gorgeous man on Earth." I held my hand further away to admire the ring from a new angle.

"Engagement rings aren't very common in Italy, so it wouldn't have been easy to find the traditional diamond but Florence was perfect for more unique designs," he said.

He turned suddenly to a couple walking by. "Mi scusi," he began, before politely asking them to take our picture. He informed them that we'd just gotten engaged and we both beamed at the congratulations. The lady took two pictures of us, one of us both smiling, me excitedly splaying my newly blinged-hand across Owen's abdomen, and another with him kissing me on the cheek.

"Je ne peux pas vivre sans toi. Tu es l'amour de ma vie et je t'aimerai de tout mon coeur pour toujours." I said. *I can't live without you. You are the love of my life and I will love you with all my heart for always.*

Owen squeezed my hands happily. Then, he cocked his head to the side. "Wait, that was French. Now we're being romantic in three languages?"

I giggled. "I love you so much, I might have to learn Spanish just to have even more words to tell you how I feel."

LA FINE
(*The End*)

ITALIAN LANGUAGE CHEAT SHEET

In case you have a special someone you'd like to seduce in Italian, here's a handy cheat sheet:

1. *Grazie*— Thanks
2. *Solo un po'*— Only a little / just a bit
3. *Buona fortuna*— Good luck
4. *Buongiorno Professore*—Hello Professor
5. *Firenze*— Florence
6. *Ti voglio bene*— I love you a lot
7. *Ti amo*— I love you
8. *Scusatemi signori*— Excuse me, gentlemen
9. *Ciao bella*— Hello pretty girl, hey girl
10. *Il mio tesoro / tesoro mio*— My treasure
11. *Pensierino per te*— A small gift/trinket for you
12. *Sei il sole della mia vita*— You are the sun of my life
13. *Tuo zelo*— Your zeal
14. *Bellissima*— Beautiful
15. *Ti amo tanto*— Much love, I love you lots
16. *Cuore mio, il mio cuore*— My heart/my dear
17. *Mi spiace*— Sorry

18. *Sei tutto per me—* You're everything to me
19. *Voglio solo pensare a te—*I only want to think of you
20. *Quel che sarà sarà—* What will be will be
21. *Sei tutto ciò che voglio—* You're all that I want
22. *Biscottino—* Cookie (pet name)
23. *Senza di te non posso più vivere—* I can't live without you
24. *Non sono niente senza di te—* I am nothing without you
25. *Per te farei di tutto—* I'd do anything for you
26. *Il mio cuore è solo tuo—* My heart is yours
27. *Si—* Yes
28. *Tu sei la mia stella—* You are my star
29. *Mi fa perdere la testa—* You make me lose my mind
30. *Cara mia, ti voglio tanto bene—* My darling, I love you so much
31. *Vorrei annegare nei tuoi occhi—* I want to drown in your eyes
32. *Mi vuoi sposare?—*Will you marry me?
33. *Voglio invecchiare con te—* I want to grow old with you
34. *Mi scusi—* Excuse me (formal)
35. *La fine—* The End

And for good measure, here's the rough translation of the French from the final chapter:

1. *Je ne peux pas vivre sans toi—* I can't live without you
2. *Tu es l'amour de ma vie et je t'aimerai toujours avec tout mon coeur—*You are the love of my life and I'll always love you with all of my heart

ACKNOWLEDGMENTS

Writing is generally a solo endeavor, but so many people have made it possible for me to achieve my dream of writing books. From the help with childcare to the random fact-checking, it truly takes a village to create these books and I appreciate all the help I've received.

Thank you Rina for looking over my Italian translations for me. I loved my Italian courses in college, but I sure have forgotten a lot!

I'm also appreciative for the folks over at Iceberg Project for their fun bite-sized Italian lessons. Check out their website if you're interested: http://icebergproject.co/italian/

Thank you to my beta-readers, critique partners, and local RWA group. I couldn't have survived this process without you all!

Thank you to my editor, Kimberly. You always strengthen my books, but somehow you also manage to make the editing process less painful.

Thank you to my cover artist, JD Book Designs. Your patience with my big ideas and your vision for the finished product is priceless.

Finally, thank you to all of the readers, bloggers, and other writers who support the literary industry and make it so fulfilling to create works of fiction. I'm filled with gratitude for the outpouring of support I've received from my fans.

ABOUT THE AUTHOR

Liza Malloy writes contemporary romance, new adult romance, women's fiction, and fantasy romance. She's a sucker for alpha males, bad boys, dimples, and muscles, and she can't resist a man in uniform. Liza loves creating worlds where the heroine discovers her own strength and finds her Happily Ever After. When Liza isn't reading or writing torrid love stories, she's a practicing attorney. Her other passions include gummy bears, jelly beans, and the occasional marathon. She lives in the Midwest with her four daughters and her own Prince Charming. *For Love and Italian* is her second published novel. She has two more steamy romances slated for release in 2019.

Visit her website at: www.LizaMalloy.com

ALSO BY LIZA MALLOY

Sixty Days for Love

She's on the clock to win him back!

Chelsea Craig's life is perfect, until her husband David runs off with his paralegal. During the mandatory sixty-day waiting period before the divorce is finalized, Chelsea decides to transform herself into a woman David can't resist. Revamping her life isn't easy, though, and Chelsea lands in one embarrassing predicament after another. Luckily, Nick, a smoldering local cop, happily rushes to her rescue. Convinced that a fling with Nick couldn't hurt, Chelsea embraces the sizzling chemistry they share. But when the separation period draws to a close, Chelsea begins to question whether she's been working all this time to salvage a relationship with the wrong man.

Available for purchase through Amazon, Barnes & Noble, Apple Books and Kobo.

Sixty Days for Love

* * *

* * *

Forbidden Ink

Loving the bad boy never felt so good!

Look for this new adult contemporary romance on July 9, 2019.

* * *

The Awakening

When worlds collide, can love truly conquer all?

The first title in this exciting new adult fantasy-romance trilogy will be available in September 2019.

Made in the USA
Lexington, KY
13 May 2019